THE POOR AND THE HAUNTED

DUSTIN MCKISSEN

Black Rose Writing | Texas

ISBN: 978-1-68433-364-6
PUBLISHED BY BLACK ROSE WRITING
www.blackrosewriting.com

Printed in the United States of America
Suggested Retail Price (SRP) $15.95

The Poor and the Haunted is printed in Calluna

For Cody and Levi.

But the stars are burnin' bright like some mystery uncovered
I'll keep movin' through the dark with you in my heart
My blood brother

THE POOR
AND THE
HAUNTED

*I'm pale as a ghost
You know what I love about you
That's what I need the most*
~Warren Zevon~

CHAPTER ONE

2019

"Why," Jessica asked, "do hauntings only happen to poor people?"

The man they watched on TV was definitely poor and definitely haunted. On their flat screen, Don Decker, the Pennsylvania Rain Man, told his story to the makers of *Paranormal Witness*. Jessica loved these shows: *Ghost Hunters, Fact or Faked, A Haunting*, even the one where the family cat could supposedly detect ghosts and demons.

Though Jimmy hated these shows, he loved spending time with his daughter. Her unshaven knees pulled to her chest, Jessica was still a child, and Jimmy's opinion still mattered to her. More time with her was worth paying just about any price, including watching the story of the Pennsylvania Rain Man.

"Do hauntings only happen to poor people?" Jimmy asked. "Is that a fact?"

"Dad. *Amityville?* The Lutzes, they were about to lose it all," Jessica said, pausing the show. "This guy here? The Rain Main? He was in jail for stealing TVs. All these shows, the families are always poor and full of stepchildren. They all have stepdads and stepmoms. Everyone is almost about to go into bankruptly. It's a thing, dad."

Jimmy did not correct his daughter's butchering of the word "bankruptcy." This increasingly rare mispronunciation was one of the fast-disappearing reminders of the baby girl he wanted since the day he and Jill got married. Jessica had a fight in her Jimmy loved even when she was a baby. Years ago, Jimmy, Jill, and her older brother, Jonathan, had to make sure the front door was shut; otherwise, Jessica—all eighteen months of her—would race outside to pick a fight with the cactus in their yard. She always lost the fight, but losses did not stop baby Jessica from going back for more.

"Did you run this theory by Mom?"

"Yep."

"What did she say?"

"She said to ask you."

"Ask me? Why?"

"She said you knew more about these things."

"What things?"

"Hauntings."

Jimmy stretched his legs out, putting his feet up on their coffee table before pulling them down and placing them back up again. He could hear the rhythmic sound of a basketball bouncing in their driveway; Jonathan was practicing for high school tryouts. Jill was off somewhere, maybe planting strawberries in their small garden in the side yard. His wife could not make herself sit still long enough to watch one of Jessica's paranormal shows, and Jonathan made Jessica feel like doing anything with her was a sentence he must grimly endure, like one of the prisoners in the *Lockup* shows he liked to watch.

Hard time and hauntings helped his children escape the cushy life Jimmy provided.

"Dad?"

"Let me think for a minute."

Did hauntings only ever happen to poor people?

He did not have an answer and wasn't sure why Jill thought he would.

"I don't know."

Jessica appreciated what her dad didn't do. He didn't tell her hauntings weren't real, or ghosts and demons are fake. Or what she was watching was trash. He considered her question and did not have an answer and respected her enough to tell her. In Jessica's eyes, taking her question seriously was the same as taking her seriously, and taking her seriously was the first hurdle any man—including her dad—had to leap before she could love them.

And Jessica loved her dad fiercely.

She snuggled her hairy knees and pointy elbows into Jimmy, and hit play. On the television, Don Decker told how, on a weekend furlough from jail in the 1980s, rain started to pour down inside the house he was staying in, which belonged to a family friend. The friend offered Don a place to stay over the weekend, so he could attend the funeral of his grandfather before returning to jail. Everywhere Don went that weekend rain poured down from the ceiling. The rain fell up, down, and sideways—like it sometimes did during an Oklahoma thunderstorm. Jimmy thought of those storms, the way the sky darkened his father's face, the burst vessels of his nose made redder by the weird shade of daylight that preceded the sound of tornado sirens.

Jimmy looked back at the TV, his arms studded with goosebumps for the first time that afternoon. He took note of the goosebumps but remained unaware of the single tear that rolled down his neck before being absorbed by his undershirt.

Though no one has ever explained what happened, Don Decker's story was corroborated by police officers and jail personnel.

Trustworthy people. Serious people.

"I love this story," Jessica said.

"Why?"

"Because it isn't typical. It's not another one of those possession stories where some girl starts cursing out Jesus and showing her privates until a priest shows up. I get tired of those. Stories like this make me believe. This one is real. It happened. You can tell by looking at his eyes."

That part was true. Don Decker's blue eyes looked almost alien as he told his story. But Jimmy didn't need to see the man's eyes to know his daughter was right. If you wanted to know whether someone was disturbed, all you needed to do was look them in the eye.

Jimmy and Jessica Lansford sat on a couch in a suburban Phoenix tract home, their house the exact same floorplan as their neighbors on each side.

It was disorienting to walk into a bizzaro version of your own home. It reminded Jimmy of watching *Stranger Things* with Jessica. Going to his neighbor's house was like visiting the Upside Down. The opposite of Jimmy's world is full of overpriced stuff from Pottery Barn, rather than overpriced stuff from Crate and Barrel—an otherworld designed by developers who consumed wild desert like The Blob in *The Blob*.

The furniture supplier of choice wasn't the sole difference between his and his neighbors' houses. In Jimmy's reality, a framed picture of his family sat on the counter next to his fridge. Six inches away sat another picture of his sister, Jessica and Jonathan's Aunt Kelly. In his neighbor's reality, the same space was occupied by a cookie jar.

Housing developments like the one the Lansfords called home were defined by two main characteristics. First, they had pompous, goofy names. The Lansfords' development was "Estancia Estates at Red Rock Ridge by KJ Homes (Units starting from the $500s!)." The other defining characteristic was the near total lack of interaction between neighbors, fueled by the disorienting sameness of every home and the eight-foot walls erected to separate yards.

Exceptions existed, of course, including the opulent birthday parties that brought the entire neighborhood together, or at least the neighbors with children.

When Jonathan was younger, he and Jimmy walked around the backyard, pretending the eight-foot walls kept them safe from monsters living outside their castle. Those days were gone. Jonathan had grown too old and too cool to play games with his dad. Now he was out in the driveway, wearing $120 Kyrie Irving shoes he bought with money he earned mowing lawns. There would undoubtedly be sweat glistening in the scraggly beard his mother hated.

Despite what Jimmy thought, Jill was not gardening. She was completing her application to work for a startup as their CFO. There were no diapers left to change, no playdates to coordinate. She wanted to put her accounting degree to use. She hung on as long as she could, believing Jonathan and Jessica needed her at home. Jill stopped believing that the first time she felt a hand on her shoulder and turned around to kiss her husband, but instead saw a younger version of him standing before her in a basketball jersey. An almost accidental French kiss with Jonathan was all it took for Jill to realize her babies were no longer babies.

The startup she was applying to would probably fail, and the money they planned to pay her was less than she could make as a shift manager at Arby's. Still, not everyone took a chance on someone who stopped working during George W. Bush's first term. Jill was grateful for the opportunity. Even if she hadn't told Jimmy.

Outside, Jonathan ignored the ice cream truck, such childish things being beneath the next Kyrie Irving. Upstairs, Jill completed her application and resume and sent it to the startup's CEO, who happened to be the cousin of a good friend from her yoga class. Jessica leaned against her father, putting her head on his shoulder. That little gesture always made him forget to breathe. He missed the first tear rolling down his cheek, but suddenly became very aware of the second. He casually reached toward his face and pretended to scratch his smooth, freshly shaved cheeks.

With tears leaking from one eye and his little girl's head on his shoulder, Jimmy Lansford watched the story of a man whose life was forever haunted by one unexplainable, horrific event.

CHAPTER TWO

Jimmy was in his room, listening to Tupac and Biggie on a mixtape his friend Brian made him. He also had to use Brian's old Walkman to listen to the tape. Unless they started putting Walkmans beneath a flashing blue light at Kmart, Jimmy was never going to afford music in his pocket.

Ronnie, Diane, Jimmy, and Kelly Lansford lived in a big, old, rundown home on the dairy his father worked at. The house was part of his father's pay, and it was huge—though not, by any definition of the word, nice. The unfinished basement was always a black and dirty swamp of standing water at least four inches deep. There were mice in the house, and an occasional bat. But the mice were the worst.

The mice respected nothing.

This past semester, Jimmy got all A's on his report card, a first for a Lansford. Knowing their mother and father didn't care, Kelly scrounged until she found enough quarters to buy him a full-size package of Oreos as a reward. She was proud of her big brother and his good grades. Oreos were a rare treat, and Jimmy ate two and put the rest in a cupboard above the fridge. He thought they would be safe there, hidden from parents who believed everything in the house belonged to them.

His parents didn't find the Oreos, but the mice did. The rodents ate all his Oreos, shredding even the packaging. Jimmy was fifteen—practically a full-grown man—and it angered him that the mice thought it was safe to eat his treasure.

Kelly interrupted Jimmy's time with Tupac and Biggie—and more important, his time away from his family—by bursting into his room.

"Try knocking!" he shouted.

Kelly was staring at him, eyes wide, hand still on the doorknob. Behind Jimmy, the wall was covered with hand-me-down posters from Brian of grunge bands Jimmy didn't like—but even Kurt Cobain's once sad and now dead face was better to look at than the house's decaying walls.

"Jimmy, did you hear that?"

He wanted his sister to leave him alone, so he explained a sound he didn't hear.

"Yeah. It was the neighbor's dog."

Kelly knew her brother was lying. The dairy was on the outskirts of town and could almost—though not quite—be called rural. Their closest neighbor was half a mile away.

"It sounded like Mom."

"It was a dog."

"Jimmy, come with me to the barn. I think I heard Mom out there."

"Fine," Jimmy said. The sooner he got this over with, the sooner he could be alone again. He loved his sister more than anything, but sometimes he just needed space from the constant circus of his home. Kelly was twelve years old, and the only good part of the circus, but like any fifteen-year-old boy, Jimmy still needed time to himself.

Jimmy and Kelly went downstairs, crossing the floor of their empty living room before exiting the front door.

They left the porch and headed toward the barn, Brian's old Walkman still in Jimmy's hand. They made it to the dirt driveway and stood between their mother's rusted-out Pontiac Firebird and the flatbed pickup truck their father used—but which belonged to the dairy—when they heard a scream. It was the worst sound either of them had ever heard, including the time their mother threatened to kill their father during what could loosely be called, at least in the Lansford home, Thanksgiving.

"Stay here," Jimmy told Kelly.

"No way! I—"

"Kelly, I'm serious. Stay here."

Jimmy took the headphones off his neck and placed them over Kelly's ears. He put the Walkman in her hands.

"I'll be back in a minute," he said. "Whatever you do, do not go into the barn. And if the door starts to open, run to the house and yell my name. Yell my name the whole time. Do you understand me?"

This was not the first time Jimmy had to come up with a plan to keep them safe, and it would not be the last.

"Jimmy," she said, looking at the barn, "I'm scared."

"Don't be scared. I got you. If the door starts to open, run. Even if someone looks hurt."

"Kay."

Kelly did not scare easy, but when she did she reverted to her elementary school vocabulary, filled with words like "Kay."

It was a sunny Saturday morning. Later Jimmy remembered how warm and bright it was, free of pitch-black clouds or summer tornado sirens, how it didn't feel like a morning for bloodcurdling screams. He squeezed Kelly's hands, looking at the spray of freckles across her nose, her shiny eyes, the thick eyebrows, her sharp jawline. He knew one day soon Brian would be just fine with Kelly tagging along.

Jimmy gave her a quick hug and ran back to the house, going up the porch stairs and through the front door. He headed straight toward Kelly's room.

To say his sister's portion of the house was messy was an understatement. There were layers to the stuff she discarded and left on her floor. In their family, Kelly was the messy one, and Jimmy was the clean one. To her credit, though, Kelly wasn't like her friends. Jimmy knew a girl her age should love boy bands and have posters on the wall of actors from *90210* or whatever it was twelve-year-old girls found interesting.

Kelly was different. Her favorite singer was Cyndi Lauper, and it wasn't long before he found the tape with "Time after Time" on it. Jimmy knew it was his sister's favorite song. He grabbed it and ran back outside.

Kelly stood in the same spot, looking toward him, rather than keeping her eye on the barn.

"You okay?" he asked.

"Yeah."

"Any more screaming while I was gone?"

"No."

Jimmy opened the Walkman, took out Tupac and Biggie, and replaced it with Cyndi Lauper. He put his hands on his sister's shoulders, looked her in the eyes, and ran his hands through her long, curly brown hair.

He kissed her on the forehead, something he hadn't done since Kelly was a little girl.

The kiss made her feel safe. The feeling of safety wouldn't last, but the feeling of being loved by her big brother did.

At twelve and fifteen, siblings are often enemy combatants for scarce resources, which is especially true for poor kids like Jimmy and Kelly. Love, encouraging words, food, and money—scarcity was the soul of the Lansford home. There wasn't enough of anything to go around. They waged war over a single Fruit Roll-up like conquistadors fighting for gold. They could, under the right circumstances, before they were separated by their parents, draw blood—but often Diane and Ronnie were too drunk or high to notice their children fighting. On most days, their mother and father were engaged in a fight over scarce resources of their own.

Usually money, but sometimes love.

The Lansford siblings were also each other's guardians. One time their father had Jimmy by the shirt, his fists ready to rid his son of his remaining baby teeth. Ronnie didn't graduate from high school, but the class ring he once accepted as payment for a dime bag could still teach his son a lesson about mouthing off to his father. But before he could start in on the lesson, Kelly leapt on her father's back, wrapped her legs around his waist, and sank her teeth deep into Ronnie Lansford's neck. The bite was deep enough her canines penetrated the sweaty flesh near her father's jugular vein.

After he shook Kelly off, her father stumbled away, blood running into the hair covering his bare chest. Jimmy never forgot the sight of his sister, dangling from their father's neck by just her teeth, growling like a rabid dog.

The Lansford children learned several lessons from their environment. One of those lessons was a promise of love and loyalty sometimes required doing whatever it takes.

And a sharp set of teeth.

They didn't protect each other from just the violent outbursts and constant warring of their parents. They protected one another from change. For the Lansfords, change of any type usually meant change for the worse. Change always left them with less than they had before, which was hard to believe, considering they started with nothing.

Jimmy understood the scream they just heard meant change, and even more so than usual, change for the worse. He raised his hands to the headphones swallowing Kelly's ears, pressed gently, squeezed her shoulders, and walked toward the barn.

Kelly pressed the headphones tighter against her ears, listening to Cyndi Lauper reassure her if she was lost, or if she fell, someone would catch her.

Time after time.

Standing between a rusted-out Firebird and a crappy old truck her dad didn't even own, the cars themselves sandwiched between a rodent-filled house and crumbling barn where she just heard a nightmare scream, she sure hoped someone would catch her and her brother.

But she doubted it.

CHAPTER THREE

2019

Over the last year, Jimmy's dislike for work travel slowly morphed into hatred.

And tears.

Often a single tear welled up in his eye before rolling down his cheek. Once he wept from just his right eye, which was strange, but not as strange as a grown man bursting into tears while running, driving alone in a rental car, or just sitting in his office, listening to music.

In his present state, he assumed the worst-possible decision he could make was holing up alone in a hotel room and ordering room service. No matter what the Cedar Rapids Marriot served, it would pale in comparison to Jill's meatloaf. Or her chicken. Or her grilled cheese. Or cereal, poured by Jill. Room service—an idea so glamorous when he was a kid—long ago lost its novelty and appeal.

He decided to skip the disappointment of a hotel meal. This Marriot was built using a design Jimmy rarely saw. The rooms surrounded an interior, indoor courtyard. Jimmy was on the second floor, and he could view the hot tub from his room.

He set his coffee cup on the windowsill, changed into his shorts, and left his room, passing the vending and ice machines near the elevator.

Jimmy entered the courtyard through a waist-high gate. He had the hot tub to himself. That was fine with him. Leaning against the jets massaging his lower back, Jimmy assumed it was sweat running down his face. He had been in the water for fifteen or twenty minutes, and it was warm. He reached up to wipe the sweat off his cheek, and realized he was crying.

Again.

Jimmy slowly lowered himself further, the top of his hair bobbing and floating beneath fizzy bubbles like a male-pattern jellyfish. He kept himself underwater for as long as he could, hoping a little heat could shake his funk.

When he emerged from the water, he looked toward his second-floor window.

There was someone in his room, watching Jimmy sob. Jimmy could feel whoever it was looking back at him. The window must have been dirtier on the outside than it was on the inside, because Jimmy could not make out the observer's face. He could not tell if it was a man or a woman. From the hot tub, the observer looked more like a human-shaped smudge than an actual person.

His observer did not appear to have any shame about being caught red-handed.

Jimmy was paralyzed, unable to do anything but look at the person standing at his window. His son Jonathan feared home invasion, having watched *The Strangers* when he was eleven. Jimmy and Jill bought an expensive alarm system just to reassure him. He was thinking about whether he should tell Jonathan this story when he realized if the observer stole his clothes he would be left with just a pair of soaking wet gym shorts.

He got out of the hot tub, grabbed his key, and ran, bumping his knee on the gate, hard enough to break skin. After Jimmy's run, the path from the hot tub to the second floor was dotted with drops of blood.

Jimmy had his hand on the door of his room when he stopped. He learned a hard lesson once in his life: Some doors are fine to go through alone. Others aren't. This one wasn't. He had no idea what the person on the other side of the door intended to do to him, or why they chose his room. He took his hand from the doorknob, stuffed his keycard back into his pocket, and ran to the lobby.

"There is someone in my room," he told the front desk clerk, a young woman in her early twenties named Brooke.

"Are you sure, Mr. Lansford?" Brooke asked. When Jimmy didn't answer, she continued. "You checked in alone, and housekeeping isn't on duty. Unless you need something, of course."

"I was down in the hot tub and I looked up and someone was in my room," he said.

"Are you sure it was your room?"

"Yes."

She looked doubtful but picked up a walkie-talkie next to her.

"Nelson?" She asked the walkie-talkie, which emitted static that sounded like "yes."

"Nelson, Mr. Lansford in room 237 believes he may have seen an unauthorized person in his room. Can—"

"Tell him I'll meet him there," Jimmy said.

"Mr. Lansford says he'll meet you there."

"Thank you," Jimmy said.

"Sure," Brooke said, looking at him for a while longer before sitting back down.

Jimmy took the stairs back to the second floor, completely oblivious to the drops of knee blood dotting the carpet. Nelson, a large man with a security badge, a shaved head, and all sorts of gadgets attached to his belt—though not a gun—was already waiting. He stuck out his hand when Jimmy was close enough, and said, "Hello. Sorry for the inconvenience, Mr. Lansford."

"Thank you. Thank you...for your help," Jimmy said, looking at the doorknob.

"Sure thing. I'm going to open up this door and go in first. Stand back and to the side, in case he's still in there."

Nelson opened the door, hand on one of his gadgets, and entered Jimmy's room. Jimmy could hear the security guard moving around the bed, opening the closet, opening the bathroom door, even opening the dresser drawers.

"Mr. Lansford?"

"Yeah?"

"Come on in here."

Jimmy entered the room. Nelson was standing next to the TV. The curtains still opened to the courtyard. Jimmy's coffee cup still sat on the windowsill.

"It doesn't look like anyone is in here," Nelson said.

"I saw someone," Jimmy said.

"I'm not saying no one was in here. It just looks like nothing was disturbed."

Other than me, Jimmy thought. Nothing disturbed in this room, other than me.

"But I saw someone," he said again.

"Could be. Could be," Nelson said. "You know, it could be a confused person. Someone off their meds."

"With a key to my room?"

"You never know," Nelson said. "These new keycards aren't like old-fashioned keys. Maybe something got crossed up in the software, and they got a key to your room."

"Thanks," Jimmy said. "Hey, do you mind if I watch the camera footage? You guys have cameras at the end of the hall, right?"

Nelson paused at the door. It was clear the security guard didn't believe anyone had been in this room, but it was also clear Nelson was a kind man and didn't want to make the night harder on Jimmy.

"Sure thing. Me and you and Brooke can crowd around the monitor and watch the footage." He paused and tried for a joke. "Maybe we'll get some popcorn."

Jimmy realized he hadn't texted Jill in a while, and grabbed his phone—and, just like he suspected, she had sent him a message.

You okay?? Haven't heard from you in a bit. Just making sure you're doing good.

She tended to check on him right when he needed checking on. He repaid his wife's thoughtfulness, perception, and love with a lie.

I'm safe babe, he texted her.

More than a thousand miles away, Jill set her phone down on their kitchen counter, not knowing what to do with that response. She waited a moment and looked at her screen again before setting the device down so she could watch reruns of *The Voice* with Jonathan and Jessica.

Downstairs, in the small room behind the front desk area, Nelson, Brooke, and Jimmy gathered around the monitor. The security system's software allowed Nelson to zoom in on Jimmy's door and scroll through all the footage recorded since Jimmy checked in.

There was Jimmy entering the room, the handle to his bag in his left hand as he used his right to open the door.

There was Jimmy leaving his room in his gym shorts, his shoulders bare and white in the camera footage.

There was Jimmy returning to room 237, soaking wet and lacking even a pool towel. He stood outside his door, his hand clenching the metal handle, the keycard still in his pocket. Even in the grainy footage it was possible to see Jimmy's eyes suddenly widen as he exited the frame at a full run.

There were Jimmy and Nelson, standing at Jimmy's door. Nelson entered the room, and shortly after Jimmy followed.

Finally, Jimmy and Nelson left the room and exited the frame to head downstairs.

Nowhere, in any of the footage, could anyone be seen entering Jimmy's room.

Nelson zoomed out and played the same footage for the two rooms on either side of Jimmy's. The only movement in the footage was Jimmy and Nelson alternately running and walking through the frames. No other guests appeared on the monitor.

"I'm sorry, Mr. Lansford," Brooke said. "Maybe you're just tired and a little hungry. Travel is hard on us all. If you want to go lie down, I could send up some complimentary room service. We have a black n' bleu burger that's pretty good, if you like bleu cheese."

"No thank you," Jimmy said. "I think I lost my appetite."

"We can put you in a different room," she offered.

"No thank you. I think I'll stay in the room Nelson already checked."

"Just let me know if you change your mind," she said.

"Mr. Lansford," Nelson said. "If you do hear anything strange, or someone tries to enter your room, just hit zero and ask for Brooke. She'll send me right away. I can come check on you, if you want. I'll also do a few walk-bys tonight."

"That'll be okay," Jimmy said.

He felt stupid and cowardly. A grown man, crying in a hot tub before panicking and getting a security guard.

"I'm just going to go up and get to bed," he said, shaking Brooke's and Nelson's hands before heading toward his room for the fourth time since he checked in. When he entered, he texted Jill again, telling her another lie.

Sorry for the radio silence! I'm just tired. Fell asleep. I think I'm going to go back to bed, and I'll call you in the morning. LY!

As soon as he set his phone down, it vibrated with a new message.

Love you too! Call me as SOON as you wake up! It's hot here! Miss you so much.

His shorts had long since dried, and he didn't bother taking them off. He was exhausted and wanted to ride this wave of fatigue right into sleep, before he could start thinking again. These days, thinking usually led to crying and crying now apparently led to hallucinations. He lay down on the bed, keeping the curtains open. The turquoise glow of the chlorinated water illuminated his room.

The light from the pool helped him see what was there on the window, what Nelson missed by checking drawers and closets:

A single handprint, in the exact spot with the best view of the hot tub.

Jimmy grabbed his phone, his bag, and one dress shoe. He took what he could and ran. He wasn't a cross-country superstar anymore, but his legs could still move. If Nelson and Brooke were watching the security footage at that moment, rather than standing outside the rear exit having a cigarette, they would see Jimmy leaving his room at a dead run toward the exit closest to his rental car.

That same night, the security cameras at Kmart recorded a man walking into the store in gym shorts, a hoodie featuring a high school basketball team's logo, and sneakers. Until that night, the man believed he and Kmart crossed paths for the last time back in the 1990s. His lack of familiarity with the store is apparent on the footage, as he wanders around aimlessly for several minutes. Wanders, in fact, might be an understatement.

The man appears lost.

After he left the store, exterior cameras recorded the same man driving a nondescript rental car toward a deserted corner of the Kmart parking lot. The car remained in the same place until 8 AM the following morning, before leaving and heading toward a Gold's Gym. There, the man showered and changed for the meeting that was the whole reason for him traveling to this town.

Jimmy would be the first to admit the meeting wasn't his best performance, but he had an excuse. He spent most of his night sitting bolt upright in a rented Nissan Altima, too scared to close his eyes.

CHAPTER FOUR

1997

Kelly stood between their parents' cars, hands squeezing the headphones covering her ears, her eyes shut. That was good. Jimmy knew there was nothing inside the barn a twelve-year-old girl should see.

They did not play around the farm. The excuse they gave themselves, each other, and their parents (when their parents cared to ask) was they were too old. Too old for tire swings. Too old to build forts. Too old to play in a dirty barn. But the main reason they didn't explore the farm was because the farm terrified them.

Jimmy had been inside the barn just once before and wasn't familiar with how the door worked. It turned out he didn't need to be. The door was already wedged open, and Jimmy easily slipped through the crack to the darkness on the other side.

Scattered daylight shone through several holes in the old and broken roof, the beams of sunshine cutting through the dust. Even with the sunlight, it took Jimmy's eyes time to adjust. When they did, he saw his mother sitting on the ground, her back to Jimmy. His mother's soft crying was interrupted by her own scream.

In scary movies, people screamed for one reason: terror. In the movies, Drew Barrymore and Neve Campbell screamed when Ghostface tried to cut their throats. The sound coming from deep inside his mother was not terror. She did not sound like Neve Campbell. This sound was something else. It was mean. Jimmy hoped Kelly had the volume on the Walkman turned all the way up.

"Mom?"

Another scream.

"MOM?"

If he heard one more wordless scream, he would turn around, get Kelly, grab the spare key to the Firebird their parents hid in the visor, and just take off. Jimmy didn't know how to drive a car. It couldn't be hard, though. His parents drove no matter how high or drunk they were, and he and Kelly were still alive. He would figure it out.

He was a big brother. He would do what had to be done. Jimmy would take his sister away from this place. They would go and make a life for themselves somewhere else.

Anywhere else.

His mother adjusted her body and looked back over her shoulder toward her son.

He wished she hadn't.

Her face, right to her hairline, was covered in blood. It looked like the facemasks Brian's mom would wear and peel off before she tucked Brian in—except you can't buy blood in the cosmetics section of JCPenney. And JCPenney didn't take payment in food stamps. Diane's lower right arm was also soaked in crimson. Jimmy tasted generic Rice Krispies rise to the bottom of his throat. He bent over to keep himself from vomiting.

Jimmy looked back up, toward his mother, and saw her legs were at an unnatural angle.

That's when he realized the legs weren't his mother's. Diane Lansford was holding a body, her own legs tucked beneath her, arms wrapped around the shoulders of whoever she mourned. Jimmy moved toward his mother. She did not appear to notice. She just rocked back and forth, her knees bouncing off the barn's dirt floor.

Jimmy saw who his mother held in her arms.

His father's feet were clad in a pair of Kmart sneakers. His legs were wrapped in Rustler jeans. He was wearing a t-shirt, though what the t-shirt had on it was a mystery. There was too much blood to tell. Jutting from his right eye was a long, rusty piece of metal. Like his wife's, Ronnie Lanford's face was a solid red mess.

His father died when the blade penetrated his orbital socket. Jimmy later learned the tool entered hard and fast enough to travel through a significant portion of his father's brain and fracture the side of his skull.

His father was balding. Or had been balding. Ronnie Lansford as a carbon-based being with a scalp and follicles was now past tense. The only remainder was his legacy. That part of Ronnie was all arsenic, and always would be. Moving her face across the bare portions of his skull, his mother let out a one-word cry, "WHY?!"

Why?

Jimmy spent the remainder of his youth asking himself that question.

Why?

Why couldn't his parents ever get their shit together? Why couldn't his father keep a job? Why couldn't they live in a normal house, in a normal neighborhood? Why did he need his little sister to defend him? Why was his father lying in his mother's arms with a piece of farm equipment buried in his eye socket? Why, if God had a plan, was this part of the plan?

His mother asked again.

"WHY?! JIMMY WHY DID THIS HAPPEN?"

Jimmy looked up. He watched a jet pass briefly over a jagged hole in the broken wood roof. The day was clear, though he wished it weren't. It was reasonable to expect death and blood in between thunderstorms on a dark day. It was terrifying to know nightmares didn't wait for the sun to fade— or for sleep to come. He looked away from the light, the airplane, and back toward his bloody heritage.

"I don't know, Mom."

It was all he could think to say, because it was the truth. He did not know why his family was dealt a bad hand. Worse, for the life of him, he could not understand why they kept coming back to the same dealer and the same table, over and over.

He wished again for his mother's scream. Just once more. He wished for something scary enough to make him run for the door, grab his sister, get in the Firebird, and take off. He needed another scream to confirm what he already knew: though just one parent died, he and Kelly were worse than alone.

They still had Diane.

Instead, she didn't scream, and he didn't leave. The three of them stuck together—for a while, at least. They left the farm and found a HUD-subsidized place back in town, where they tried to be a family. They didn't put a lot of effort into this new family (and, other than Jimmy and Kelly, no one put a lot of effort into the old family), but they tried to stay together.

And they were all worse off for it.

CHAPTER FIVE

2019

Standing in his backyard, Jimmy remembered Jessica's first birthday party.

Back then he was still in business school. Jonathan was a toddler, and they lived in a drywall box small enough to make learning to love a close family a requirement. In those days, no one pooped alone, and though awkward at first, a pooping pal grows on you—or at least it did in the Lansford sequel, which, based on the first scene alone, was obviously a much better story than the original.

Jessica loved balloons—her first word was "BA-woon"—so Jill went overboard on the balloons. This was the daughter they always wanted, and their last first birthday party until they became grandparents.

Jill asked Jimmy to pick up the balloons from a Party City a couple of miles away from their apartment. When Jimmy arrived in the used Toyota Camry they owned back then, the clerk laughed and said, "Really?"

"Yes, really," Jimmy said.

Jill bought far too many balloons to fit in the Camry. Jimmy drove home with his arm outside the window, holding the balloons as they floated above the car. Several times during the drive back to their apartment he thought he would lose his arm, the balloons, or both.

The pain in his arm and the laughter from the neighbors were worth it. Jessica spent the entire party with her head bent back, looking toward the ceiling and saying "BA-WOON!" Balloons filled their apartment for weeks. The four of them spontaneously broke into random games of catch and balloon volleyball, Jessica crawling and mauling pink helium bubbles while

Jonathan laughed until he peed. A house full of people he loved, balloons, and constant laughter—Jimmy cried once or twice then too, but those tears differed from the tears he cried now.

Once Jimmy graduated with his MBA and earned a good salary (and then a better salary), every birthday became a bigger production, with a different theme.

A Backyardigans pool party.

A Hannah Montana Hollywood movie theatre party.

A murder mystery party, complete with costumes.

This year, for Jessica's twelfth birthday, Jill talked him into hiring a band from Jonathan's high school, which managed to send a backyard full of twelve-year-old girls into hysterics. Jimmy stood near the sliding glass door sipping a Coke and thinking about how different this party was from anything he experienced as a child.

He and Kelly never got real birthday parties. They were lucky if either one of their parents remembered their birthdays at all.

Once, when he was six, Jimmy was invited to a friend's party at the local McDonald's. When everyone else was on the playground, including adults, he put his fingers in the birthday cake. It wasn't enough to ruin the afternoon, but it was enough for Jimmy to leave his mark on the party.

Later he felt ashamed and told his father. He wanted to be punished for what he did. He wanted to be told he let everyone down.

Instead, his father laughed and said, "Fuck 'em. Fuck 'em. That'll teach 'em." At six, Jimmy wasn't sure what ruining the birthday cake would teach his friend, other than to never invite Jimmy Lansford to a party again.

His childhood memories were interrupted by his neighbor, Bill, who sidled up without Jimmy even noticing. Bill was one of the few neighbors Jimmy regularly spoke with.

"Goes by fast, doesn't it?" Bill asked.

"It does, it does go by fast. A lot faster than we think."

"Yep," Bill said. "Hot outside, isn't it?"

It is Phoenix, Jimmy thought. Commenting on the heat was like looking at a tomato and saying, "Sure is red, isn't it?"

"Yep," Jimmy said. "But you know what they say. It's a dry heat."

"Dry heat! Ha! Yeah. So is an oven."

"Yep. Ovens are hot," Jimmy said.

Jimmy preferred small talk to deep conversations. He couldn't do it today, though. He couldn't pretend the most important thing on his mind was the heat or the Diamondbacks pitching staff.

"Can I tell you something, Bill?" Jimmy asked. He ran his hand through the sweaty remains of his hair.

"Sure thing, buddy," Bill said.

Jimmy looked at the collection of strangers in his backyard. Superficially, they were human Old Navy: visually inoffensive, totally unmemorable, straight off the rack. Superficially, he was no different. But deep down, he knew there was more to his neighbors than they presented at a suburban birthday party. What he was looking at was just a collection of storefronts.

Even Old Navy has skeletons in its closet.

Or ghosts.

"I...I think I saw a ghost. In an airport Marriot. On a trip to Cedar Rapids."

Jimmy had lived next to Bill for years, and he knew there were a limited number of subjects Bill found worthy of conversation. Ghosts were not on the list of preapproved topics.

Maybe it was the heat. Maybe it was his daughter turning twelve. It's always difficult to see your kids leave childhood behind, but this birthday was uniquely difficult, and his ability to maintain a conversation about the heat he and Bill shared a hundred times before was gone.

Bill stared at him, soda halfway to his lips, until he said, "I...really? Mary watches ghost shows all the time. I...guess I don't believe in that stuff."

"I was in the hot tub, in the hotel courtyard, when I saw someone staring back at me from my room. I got the security guard to take a look, and he didn't see anything. But I did. I saw it."

Bill looked panicked. That the conversation deviated at all from their normal list of topics was bad enough, but ghosts?

"Cedar Rapids," Bill said. "Huh. I don't know about ghosts, but I think the city has a minor league team. They're an affiliate of the Cards, right? No, the Twins? No, the Cubs. No, no. It's the Twins. No, I think it's the Reds."

This listing of baseball teams would have gone on for quite a while had Jimmy not grabbed the soda from Bill's hand, raised it to his own lips, and finished it.

"Like I said, the security guard checked the room and found nothing—no one. Not a thing. We watched the security camera footage, and you couldn't see anything on that either," Jimmy said. "So, I went back to the room. There was a handprint on the window. I left...I...I went to Kmart."

There was a long moment of silence before Bill said, "Kmart? I didn't know they still had those. Remember when you were a kid, and your mom took you to get some toys when there was...what did they call that? The red something sale?"

"The Blue Light Special," Jimmy said.

Jimmy never shopped for toys under the blue light. Instead, he remembered Diane buying Spam, Cheese Whiz, and generic white bread. A complete meal, illuminated by one half of a knockoff police siren.

Jimmy, Bill, and the collection of storefronts gathered in the Lansford backyard understood suburbs are a tradeoff of safety for conformity, variety for comfort. That afternoon Jimmy lost his ability to conform, and Bill lost his sense of comfort.

"Have a good day, Jimmy," Bill said. "And tell Jessica I said happy birthday."

"Bye, Bill."

"And tell her I said not to grow up. It goes by too fast."

Bill walked away, looking for his wife. Looking for an excuse to leave the party.

Jimmy already regretted making Bill feel uncomfortable. Being kind was something he prioritized. Kindness was not a character trait valued by Jimmy's parents, and he defined himself and his version of the Lansfords in response to his family of origin.

He went through the sliding glass door and made his way to the half bathroom on the first floor, needing to relieve himself of a bladder full of Coca-Cola.

After he did his business, he stopped to look in the mirror. He stared at his own reflection. He was starting to lose his hair, the lines across his forehead deepening every year. Every month, lately.

He was still a good-looking man, but he was no longer a young-looking man.

For most of his life he could ignore it, but at the early onset of middle age, it was unavoidable: He looked more and more like Ronnie Lansford every day, but when Ronnie died, his face was weathered by rage and Marlboro Reds—not the smile lines that aged Jimmy's face. But the hair, the nose, the cheekbones, the chin, the coloring, the ear size—all the fleshy ghost of Ronnie Lansford.

And the eyes.

Jimmy, without question, owned his father's eyes.

The same heavy lids.

The same blue.

Jimmy stepped closer toward the mirror. Suddenly he wanted to dart left, just to see if the man in the mirror did the same. For some reason, he doubted it. Instead, he pulled back the lids of his right eye with two fingers.

The man in the mirror pulled back his lids, too.

Suddenly he felt pressure across the entire backside of his body. He stood there with his right eye still pulled open.

He felt light wind, neither hot nor cold, on his neck. The light bulbs in the fixture above the sink glowed steadily brighter, until one burned out. The mirror was dirty, smudged just above his shoulder. He reached toward the mirror and touched the smudge. His entire arm went cold. The backyard BBQ he consumed traveled up his throat, out his mouth, and into the sink. He removed his hand from the mirror and felt whatever it was leave the room.

The pressure on the backside of his body was gone.

Jimmy washed his face and rinsed his mouth out before turning the faucet off. He stayed there, stooped over. He ran his tongue along his teeth, the canines sharp and bone-white. Jimmy placed his tongue between his teeth and bit down, bright red staining a mouth full of Blue Cross/Blue Shield-covered alabaster.

If Jimmy recapped the day as honestly as he could (though he would not do that, not even to Jill), he would say he was talking with his neighbor, perhaps even joking, when he realized he needed to go inside because of the heat. There he vomited in the sink.

If Jimmy's observer recapped the events of the day, here's what it would tell you:

In the suburbs of Phoenix, a man stands in his backyard drinking a Coke. His neighbor, someone the man knows relatively well, stands by him attempting small talk. The man skips the small talk and tells a strange story about a ghost he thought he saw in Cedar Rapids.

The man turns away from his neighbor to enter his home, where he makes his way to the restroom. He stares at himself in the mirror for several minutes. The man's hair is a sweaty mess, pasted to his forehead by the perspiration that comes even during a dry heat.

Once near the mirror—so close his nose almost touches the glass—the man pulls his right eyelids apart, stretching them as far they will go. The man observes his own eye, staring straight ahead, before touching the mirror. While looking at whatever he sees over his shoulder, the man spontaneously vomits, and then bites his own tongue until drops of blood splatter the spotless sink. After vomiting, the man removes his hand from the mirror and begins scrubbing his face and rinsing his mouth out.

Most troublingly, the man remains bent over for quite some time, his teeth bared at the sink, even as everyone gathers to sing Happy Birthday.

CHAPTER SIX

1997

Who made sure Kelly got dressed and ready for school when she was too little to do it herself? Jimmy. If he didn't do it, no one else would. Who put a blanket over his mother or father when one or both passed out on the front porch, too wasted to make it to their bed?

Jimmy.

In the Lansford home, normal was not an option, and Jimmy faced two choices: Let life eat him and Kelly alive, or shoulder more of the burden than any child should. If he saw something needing cleaning, which in their house was everything—drunks and drug addicts make lousy housekeepers—Jimmy cleaned it.

But store-brand Pine-Sol could only mask so much, and lemon-fresh rot was still rot.

Standing there in the interior shadows of a ruined barn as his mother clutched his father's bloody body, Jimmy knew generic Pine-Sol—even mixed with a little bleach—could not clean this mess up.

"Mom," he said.

"Ronnie! Oh, Ronnie. RONNIE!" his mother cried.

Like Jimmy, Ronnie Lansford did not have a proper name. Ronnie was not short for Ronald. Jimmy was not short for James. Even if Jimmy never went to a good college, never bought a nice house and a new car, and never married a pretty wife, he swore if he ever had a son, he would give him a proper name.

And he would never, ever shorten his son's name.

"Ronnie! RONNIE! FUCK YOU! Ronnie!" his mother screamed, still rubbing her face on his father's bloody scalp.

"Mom?"

Nothing.

The barn was still, and when his mother wasn't wailing, quiet enough he could hear mice running back and forth in the hayloft. These mice were likely cousins of the sons of bitches who stole Jimmy's Oreos. He had a vision of walking toward his father's body, yanking the blade from his eye socket, and climbing the stairs to the hayloft before going full Lizzie Borden on every mouse he saw.

Mouse parts flew through his imagination, going so high white underbellies and pink tails shot through plane engines, raining blood on the Lansford's borrowed patch of Oklahoma cow pasture. The sky would darken, and Jimmy would be the one to darken it.

"MOM! LISTEN TO ME!"

His mother looked toward him. She was still—despite all the fried county commodity food, crystal meth, and hard liquor she consumed; despite the occasional beating she endured at the hands of Ronnie Lansford—a beautiful woman. Diane's Farrah Fawcett face could not be beaten, smoked, snorted, injected, or drunk away. Other than money, his mother's looks were the biggest reason for his parents' constant battles.

"Mom, I'm going—I'm going to call the cops."

Before his mother could say no, Jimmy slipped through the darkened crack and back into the light of the world. Kelly still stood between the cars, eyes closed, hands on the headphones, mouthing the words to "Time after Time."

Jimmy could bring Kelly back to the house while he made the call. He could hold her hand as they walked inside. She could sit next to him, on a kitchen chair, while he told the dispatcher, "I think my father's dead."

That wasn't true though.

He did not "think" his father was dead. He knew his father was dead. He had to say, "My father is dead." The dispatcher would ask how he knew, and Jimmy would say, "Because he's lying in our barn with a knife sticking out of his eye socket."

As her big brother, Jimmy could not let Kelly learn about Ronnie by eavesdropping on a conversation with a 911 dispatcher. He would have to tell her as they ran toward the house, and she might cry, and he would stop what he was doing to comfort her, and they would lose precious time. Losing time wasn't about his father living or dying. Even if his father had a chance—which he did not—Ronnie Lansford's life wasn't the most pressing reason to get someone with authority out to the dairy. Someone who carried something stronger than knockoff Pine-Sol.

Jimmy left Kelly where she was, listening to her favorite song. He would make the 911 call. All he needed to tell the dispatcher was his address, and his father had something big, sharp, and rusty sticking out of his eye.

And to please come.

Fast.

Please.

Please.

Then, he would hang up the phone, run back outside, and tell his sister what happened. He would focus on Kelly and wait for the police to deal with his mother. Jimmy ran around the front side of the Firebird, heading toward the small dirt path splitting the tall, fire ant-infested weeds they called a yard. He ascended the short wooden staircase on their front porch and stopped for a moment. Before going inside, he turned away from their front door, his hand still on the rusty old doorknob, and looked back at his sister.

It's okay, Jimmy thought. It will be okay, it will be okay, it will be okay, it will be okay, okay—

Diane screamed again.

Jimmy stepped inside the house and headed to the kitchen, where the rotary phone hung from the wall. It was more accurate to call their kitchen a "phone room," since their parents rarely cooked anything more than fried Spam and Cheez Whiz sandwiches.

Jimmy picked up the phone and dialed, looking around the crumbling kitchen and rotting wallpaper. This home, Jimmy knew, had been coming apart long before he and Kelly arrived.

"9-1-1," the female voice answered. "What is your emergency?"

"I think—I know my father's dead."

"Repeat yourself, honey."

"My father is dead."

"How do you—"

"He has a knife or something coming out of his eye a big knife it might be a piece of farm equipment I'm not sure please send someone now please send someone please please—"

"Honey, how old are you?"

"Fifteen."

"Is your mother there?"

Jimmy could hear the chaos surrounding the dispatcher.

"She's with my father."

"Is your mother alive? Is she okay?"

"She has blood all over her she's not okay but I don't think she's hurt—"

"Honey, slow down. Can you confirm your address for me?"

"71657 Torrance Road. We're in the farmhouse at the dairy."

"The Torrance Dairy?"

"Yes."

"We'll send someone out. Please, don't—"

Jimmy saw his blood-soaked mother staggering toward the house, like a zombie from *Night of the Living Dead*. This wasn't as alarming as what he couldn't see: Kelly no longer stood between the Firebird and the truck. Jimmy dropped the phone, knowing whatever the dispatcher was going to tell him wasn't half as important as finding his sister. He ran back out the front door, passing his mother on her way up the porch stairs. They exchanged no words, didn't even bother with a meaningful glance.

He ran toward the barn, going so fast he failed to hear the crunch beneath his feet as his dirty, cheap sneakers crushed the Walkman Kelly left on the ground.

Once inside, what Jimmy saw was, in a way, even worse than what he saw the first time he entered the barn. His father was flat on his back, the gaze in his one intact eye directed straight toward the sunlight coming through the holes in the roof. The knife in his other eye socket remained.

Kelly stood with her back to her brother, facing her father's body. She squatted down and used her right hand to pick up a rock from the barn's dirt floor. She stood up, cocked her right hand back, and threw the rock toward their father. Kelly was not a coordinated girl, but rage gave her an ease of movement she otherwise lacked. Jimmy saw it the time she bounded into his room and sank her teeth into their father's neck.

The rock connected, bouncing off the side of their father's head with a thud. He didn't move. Kelly might as well have thrown a rock at a package of ground beef. Stooping down again, Kelly grabbed another rock, spun, and threw it the opposite direction, toward the door his mother just exited. Jimmy ducked as the rock flew over his hunched body and hit the wall, kicking up dust and hay when it landed.

Kelly stopped when she saw Jimmy. Her face collapsed, as though everything behind it disappeared: her rage, her spark, the fight Jimmy so loved.

"Kelly I'm so sorry Kelly I'm sorry I'm sorry I'm sorry I'm sorry," he said as he took her in his arms.

Jimmy stood there, holding his sister tight. He began to hear sirens in the distance. Kelly's eyes were closed; her face pressed against Jimmy's chest. Jimmy looked at his father's body and wished harder than he ever wished for anything before. He didn't wish for his father to stand up and shake it off. He didn't want to see Ronnie stand, grab the handle, pull, and sneer from one healthy eye socket while saying, "Stop your fucking sniveling, ya pussies, or I'll give you something to cry about."

He wished Kelly didn't have to see what she was looking at. He wished he could shield his little sister from the hard realities of the world.

It was too late, though.

Jimmy held Kelly and opened his own eyes as wide as he could.

He hoped if he took as much of this scene in as possible, perhaps God would allow Kelly to unsee the grotesque sight of their father. His family didn't attend church, and Jimmy himself was ambivalent about religion, but he hoped God could find it in His heart to do him this one favor.

This one solid, as boys his age said.

The detective who entered the barn first, the detective who later gave Kelly and Jimmy the package of M&Ms in his car, noted in his report that upon walking into the barn he saw a male teenager, approximately fifteen or sixteen, holding a young female, approximately eleven or twelve. They were roughly twenty feet away from the body of a deceased adult male.

Though he did not note it in his report, the detective noticed the way the young boy stared at his father's body. He didn't seem to blink as he fixed his eyes on the dead man in threadbare Rustlers.

The detective also collected a bloody suicide note from the young female and bagged it for evidence.

Inside the house, investigators found several items of interest: discarded bags containing what the detective considered hell's unmelted snowflakes, all sorts of pipes and smoking devices, and a loaded handgun, which was curious. A bullet is a far more efficient and less painful way to commit suicide than shoving a rusty piece of farm equipment into your eye. The police also noted the infestation of mice evident throughout the house. The detective made a mental note that the house was almost devoid of food and contained little evidence a family with two children occupied the residence, with the exception of a report card filled with A's the detective found stuck to a fridge.

The detective made special note of the report card.

Upstairs, the detective found Jimmy and Kelly's mother, still covered in their father's blood, lighting up a pipe full of crystal. Unlike their father, their mother was still alive, although she was doing her best to change that. By the time the detective found her, she had smoked so much meth she might go into cardiac arrest soon, though the detective suspected she wouldn't die. It wasn't just her beauty that was resilient. She was a survivor.

Like most people who knew Diane Lansford, he came to believe resiliency was one of her worst traits.

Looking out at the two children huddled together in his cruiser, the young girl asleep with her head on her brother's shoulder, detective Mike Carlisle knew these children were better off being raised by almost anyone else. And knowing the court system as he did, he knew despite the scene before him today—one parent dying a horrific death, the other parent being found with a pipe in her mouth right as her children were processing their father's suicide—the courts wouldn't remove these children from the care of their mother. In the eyes of the court, the addict never gets better by taking his or her children away.

The judges said the health and welfare of the children were their first priority. But judges, Carlisle learned, were by and large lazy and full of shit. Family court judges knew the fastest way to get through their docket was to side with shitbag parents rather than consider the best interests of the children.

On the way to the police station—after all the M&Ms were eaten—the Detective stopped at Derry's, an ice cream place on the edge of town, near the Section 8 homes and apartments. Jimmy didn't order anything. Kelly got a chocolate-dipped cone. Jimmy said nothing during the entire drive. He looked out the window, his arm around his sister.

It appeared to the drive-thru staff at Derry's that Detective Mike Carlisle arrested two children and then stopped on his way to jail to buy them ice cream.

Carlisle looked out his window, the cruiser's flashing lights illuminating the early evening as they drove down a darkened two-lane road toward the station. Earlier, another emergency vehicle raced down the same road, its lights and sirens disrupting the stillness of a quiet Saturday afternoon. The ambulance was headed for the hospital, carrying Jimmy and Kelly's mother.

On their way into town, Carlisle looked at the stoic young boy and chocolate-stained little girl occupying the same space in his cruiser usually reserved for methheads and thieves.

Detective Mike Carlisle tried his best not to cry.

Detective Mike Carlisle did not succeed.

CHAPTER SEVEN

2019

Jimmy stood in a storage unit not far from his home in North Phoenix and thought of the last month.

He knew the handprint in Cedar Rapids hadn't come from his own hand. Something had been in his hotel room. Though he couldn't explain it, he didn't doubt it for a second.

That didn't mean he was ready to share his experience with others. He tried with Bill at Jessica's birthday party. Now, Bill likely thought he was a madman. He learned his lesson after that conversation. When Jill found him in the bathroom during Jessica's birthday, facedown and snarling at a sink stinking of his own vomit, he explained himself with excuses he knew she didn't buy.

"It's the heat," he told Jill as she stood outside the bathroom door.

"It's a dry heat," Jill said.

"But it still gets to me," he said, looking at the black suede swoosh on the side of his foot.

His explanation may or may not have convinced Jill, but it didn't convince himself. Something was in the bathroom with him. He saw the smudge just above the reflection of his own shoulder. He felt the cold shock when he touched the mirror. He sensed pressure on his back as he stared into his own eyeball. He could act like one of those tough guys in the haunting shows Jessica watched and find a thousand different ways to explain away what he experienced, but it wouldn't work.

Something had arrived, and if he wanted to learn more about who or what it was, the cardboard box full of tragedy in his storage unit was a good place to start.

Not everything in the box was terrible. Inside were items that made him smile: The choker and butterfly clips Kelly wore when she was a teenager. A single, well-used pair of white Nike running shoes. A few cross-country medals and ribbons from high school. Jimmy could run a long, long way— and fast.

Running was easy.

He would pull the handle on the spotlight in his mind, the glowing beam illuminating a cow-shit-smelling patch of Oklahoma, a crumbling barn rising from scrubland like an unmarked blood-red pauper's grave, and his legs became the wheels on Clyde Barrow's 1934 Ford.

For the most part, though, what was stored in the box was awful. The yellowed government-issued pages that documented and confirmed his father's death. The knockoff Kmart Reeboks Ronnie Lansford wore the day he died. The nasty, incoherent letters his mother wrote to his father in the year or two after his death, letters Jimmy found and hid before Kelly could read them.

All these horrors and more, including his father's suicide note.

The day of their father's death, their mother handed Kelly the note in the driveway, kicking Kelly's foot to get her attention away from the Walkman.

"Here," she said, placing Ronnie's note in Kelly's hand. She looked around at a house that belonged to someone else. She looked at a young girl she wished belonged to someone else. She looked at two fists full of her own chewed fingernails, her chemical hunger driving her to consume her own body after she ran out of Spam to chew on.

"Motherfucker don't want none of this," Diane said before going inside the house and attempting to meth herself to death. Years later, Kelly repeated the phrase as a joke, and though they should have cried, they laughed. Poor kids do that: laugh when they should cry, and cry when they should laugh.

At Arizona State, with access to the Internet, Jimmy relentlessly Googled suicide notes to see how his father's letter stacked up against the last words of others who took their own lives.

Google confirmed what Jimmy already knew: Like every syllable that ever tumbled from his rotted jaws, Ronnie Lansford's last words didn't amount to much.

IM SORRY I CANT DO THIS ANYMORE THERE IS SOMETHING WRONG INSIDE OF ME I CAN FEEL IT ITS ALWAYS BEEN THERE IT WILL BE BETTER WHEN IM GONE - RONNIE

One long sentence, unbroken by punctuation. When the police arrived, Detective Carlisle took the note from Kelly and bagged it for evidence. While suicide by impaling oneself through the eyeball is exceptionally rare, the police—though suspicious at first—concluded his father's death was suicide and released all evidence back to Jimmy's mother.

The day Jimmy got the call to pick up his father's belongings, their mother was gone. Not knowing what else to do, Mike Carlisle brought the sealed evidence bag over to the Lansford house and gave it to Jimmy.

Disappearing was something Diane did often. One minute their mother was home, the next minute she would vanish for three days on a Taco Bell run. Though Jimmy and Kelly knew she was nowhere near a Taco Bell, they were still disappointed when their mother returned with a pair of dilated pupils and zero Gorditas.

Jimmy never returned his father's belongings to his mother, choosing instead to hide the box on the top shelf of the closet he and Kelly shared. In the twenty-two years since his father killed himself, Jimmy focused on one line in his father's note: *I CANT DO THIS ANYMORE.*

Do what? Jimmy used to think. Hold down a job some of the time? Chug vodka? Fire up a glass pipe? Beat the shit out of Diane for not having the good sense to swallow the birth control pills that could have left him the plains-running stallion he imagined himself to be? What was so hard about Ronnie Lansford's life that he just couldn't go on? Nothing, as far as Jimmy knew. Now, though, Jimmy focused on another line:

THERE IS SOMETHING WRONG INSIDE OF ME I CAN FEEL IT

What did his father mean? Was it cancer? Was he using crystal and vodka to dull an actual physical pain? Or were the drinks and drugs Ronnie's way of treating schizophrenia, or bi-polar disorder, or some other mental illness? Jimmy did not know. The only person who knew died when Jimmy was twenty-five. It wasn't suicide, or murder, or an accidental overdose. Diane's liver quit on her. What her clear complexion and naturally curvy body could survive eventually became too much for her internal organs.

When he was twenty-five, he got the call from Mike Carlisle. Diane was found dead in her trailer. Like his father's last words, Diane's ashes were kept in the large cardboard box.

He could ask his mother's ashes what lurked inside his father, but there wouldn't be much in the way of a worthwhile answer. The container of ashes was about as helpful as the woman was while still alive. She gave her perspective on his father's death once, when she told Kelly "Motherfucker don't want none of this." In all her remaining years, it was the most insightful thing she ever said about the violent drifter she promised to love and honor until the day they died.

It was up to Jimmy to find out what his father meant by "SOMETHING WRONG INSIDE OF ME."

He had a theory. It was an idea he long ago dismissed as the thoughts of a young boy trying to rationalize an event lacking any rationale at all. His theory, crazy as it was, brought more comfort than the idea he shared DNA with a ticking time bomb whose last will and testament bequeathed a ninety-day late notice from Oklahoma Gas & Electric and a lifetime of bad memories.

The theory revolved around two facts:

First, his father was physically weak, despite his constant bragging about kicking someone's ass. Ronnie avoided any labor he wasn't paid to do, and his laziness showed in his concaved chest and nonexistent triceps.

Once, during a checkup at the free county health clinic for a potentially sprained ankle his senior year, Jimmy asked the doctor, "Can I ask you something?"

"Sure."

"It's sort of strange. The question I'm about to ask."

The physician, a youngish man with Chandler Bing's haircut and Danny Devito's stature, rested his clipboard on the counter across from the bed Jimmy sat on, and said, "You're in luck. All we get are strange questions."

"Okay. How strong would someone have to be to stab themselves in the eye hard enough to fracture their skull?"

Jimmy's doctor smiled and looked him in the eyes.

"I have to give you credit. That's a weird way to mess with your doctor."

"I'm not messing with you. It's a real question."

The doctor stopped smiling.

"Why are you asking? Jimmy, have you thought about hurting yourself?"

"No. My father committed suicide by stabbing himself in the eye in our barn. He—we lived on a farm. A dairy, actually. When I was a kid."

"I'm sorry, Jimmy. I think I remember reading something about that."

The doctor noted Jimmy saying, "When I was a kid." It was clear this young man experienced far more, and far worse, in just eighteen years than most people do in a lifetime.

"It's okay," Jimmy said. "I just needed...I just have always wondered."

"Okay. Well. The human body...every human body is different, but I will say it would not be an easy thing to do. First of all, your body has a natural protective instinct when it comes to your eyes. We have eyelashes and eyebrows to protect the eye from foreign objects. Being able to swing a sharp object at your eye and penetrate it, without stopping yourself before it enters, is surprising. I've never heard of anyone committing suicide like that."

"Me neither."

"Did your father have problems with drugs or alcohol?"

"Vodka...and crystal meth."

"Stabbing yourself in the eye sounds like a crystal meth thing, but even then, I haven't heard of it," the doctor said. Jimmy looked at his nametag. Dr. Paul, it said. Jimmy didn't know if that was his first or last name and didn't want to ask. "Anyway, he got it in there hard enough to fracture his skull?"

"Yep. Went in at an angle. Fractured right here," Jimmy said, knocking on the right side of his skull, above his ear.

"I guess with momentum he could do it, in theory. But it would take some strength. Some significant strength."

Strength Jimmy believed an atrophied addict and alcoholic did not have.

"Thank you, doctor."

"Jimmy, do you need to talk to someone? We don't have a counselor here at the clinic, but I can make a referral, pull some strings."

"Thank you, but I'm okay. I have this under control. I just needed to know."

"Sure? It's not a problem."

"No, I'm good."

Dr. Paul's questions made Jimmy feel less like the confident, capable young man he tried to project to the world. He felt more like the lost little boy he was.

"Gotta go," Jimmy said, and limped out of the clinic. He took Dr. Paul's prescription for Vicodin out of courtesy, knowing he would throw it in the trash as he exited the clinic. Tossing the script for high-powered pain killers in the trash was fifty percent self-preservation, fifty percent self-awareness, and one hundred percent fuck you to his greedy, chemically addled mother.

The doctor couldn't do much for his ankle, but he confirmed what Jimmy already thought he knew: His father likely wasn't strong enough to kill himself in the manner he chose.

The second leg of Jimmy's theory was the choice of method. To Jimmy, there was suicide—and there was murdering yourself. Suicide was a relatively peaceful exit. It was a belt tied to the rack in your closet, a closed garage door and a running car, a bottle of pills, a bullet to the head. Murdering yourself was something else: An act of rage taken out on your physical being, in some ways no different than killing someone else.

Ronnie Lansford didn't commit suicide.

Ronnie Lansford murdered himself.

So, Jimmy thought, why would anyone murder themselves? And in such a barbaric way? When he was eighteen, Jimmy thought he knew, but thinking about possession made Jimmy feel like just another lunatic Lansford.

Now, he wasn't so sure his theory had been crazy. Now he thought there might be something to the idea that the devil had a favorite family. Just as he grabbed the bag containing his father's note, the overhead bulb flickered twice and burst. Tiny shards of glass showered his unit like rain in Don Decker's Pennsylvania living room.

There was static in the air, the feeling of a television on with no sound— and no light. The hair on his neck and arms rose. The moisture in his nose and throat evaporated. His eyeballs felt like they would pop, their capacity to ingest the darkness around him expanding as his pupils breached the borders of his sockets.

"Hello?" Jimmy asked, his voice echoing in the dark space.

"Hello?"

He reached for the wall and grasped nothing but a fistful of vacant black.

"Who's there? Hello?"

The concrete floor beneath his feet suddenly gave way.

Jimmy floated up and up. Though he could not see any of it, he felt the storage unit, his home, his adopted city, his family, the hand towels and fresh organic soaps of his bathroom, his daily run, his beautiful carefully constructed storefront of ordinary disappear in the miles and then planets and then universes beneath him. Jimmy rose and rose and rose and rose until even a father with a rusty knife for an eye and an Oklahoma possum carcass for a heart became less than the speck of dust Carl Sagan spoke of.

He floated out past the light of the last star, out past the edge of God's creation where the only thing left to see are memories careening off the interior edges of your skull, a mad pinball game that requires no quarters and never ends.

Jimmy stretched his jaw, gathering the air in his organs and torso to scream his way back to the bright—and with his mandibles stretched wide and the scream racing upward past the red fibers of his heart, he felt the ground beneath his feet solidify.

He reached for the door, and found what he needed:

A little bit of light.

***

There were security cameras all over the halls of the storage facility, but none in the units themselves. Still, despite the lack of cameras, just off Deer Valley Road in North Phoenix, a man was observed in a single small storage unit repeating the words, "Hello" and "Who's there?" before standing for some time in the darkness, his mouth open wide as he swallowed the dark. He left, carrying a bag containing a piece of paper, still crunchy from dried blood two decades old.

The man left the storage unit and returned to the suburban home where he lived with his wife and two children. After dinner, the man was observed going back to his car and grabbing the bag he brought home from the storage unit. He placed it on a high shelf inside the garage, where his children could not reach it. He opened the door that connected the garage to the rest of the home and returned to his family for their Thursday night sitcoms.

As the door closed with a soft click, the man's observer placed its form against the door, sensing the trees that birthed the wooden particles surrounding the brass handle, the machine-cooled air inside the home, the carpet thick like the fur of the four-thousand-dollar puppies purchased in pet stores in upscale malls just a few miles away, the four people on the couch, their skin, the red and white cells traveling their veins, double-helixes half-borrowed from damaged generations before, hopefully diluted and diluted and diluted and diluted and diluted and diluted and diluted and diluted until all that was left was built here, in this new and still blank part of the country, on this couch, in interlocked fingers and pink-socked feet propped on thighs and the sound of laughter from the throat of the man who, for a moment, on a Must-See-TV Thursday night, forgot the need for a scream so deep it would leave his vocal chords ruptured like strings on an abused guitar.

CHAPTER EIGHT

1998

Three weeks after Ronnie Lansford died, Diane, Jimmy, and Kelly moved into a rundown two-bedroom government-subsidized home not far from Derry's Ice Cream Shop. Despite what had happened at the dairy, they didn't choose to leave. The Torrances told them they couldn't afford to keep the family on the property without Ronnie Lansford's labor.

"We feel for you," said Jim Torrance, standing on the porch of the farmhouse. "We really do. Just, you know, the economy. There was that whole meltdown in Asia...you saw, right?"

Torrance looked at Diane and away from the children while he said it, assuming the ragged band of leftover Lansfords would take his word for it. Jimmy knew better. He read the *USA Today* in the school library as often as he could. He knew the economy was fine. The Torrances wanted crazy Diane and her damaged offspring gone, and if it took implying a raft of porchfront bullshit about how collapsing share prices of cell phone companies in Thailand impacted milk futures in the American Midwest, they would do it. Jimmy couldn't stop them, nor did he really want to. He was done with life on the dairy—but he didn't have to buy an excuse premised on the idea that wearing secondhand shoes and being ignorant are the same thing.

While Kelly and Jimmy were happy to move back into town, the downside was sharing a bedroom—something unnatural for even the closest of opposite sex twelve- and fifteen-year-old siblings.

They made do and told no one at school they shared a room.

Detective Mike Carlisle was somewhat of a regular at Derry's, which wasn't surprising given his frequent visits to the Section 8 part of town. He pulled a few strings—small business owners in the bad part of town understood the value of a friendly relationship with the police—and got Jimmy an afterschool job running an ancient milkshake machine and learning how to turn a vanilla ice cream cone upside down and dip it in chocolate without dropping the whole thing.

His job at Derry's made Jimmy the sole worker in his home.

Diane qualified for Temporary Assistance for Needy Families, though the new law passed by the government two years prior meant her time on welfare was limited, and the state required her to actively look for a job or attend classes. Of course, the government could pass legislation, conduct a ceremonial signing, pat itself on the back, and point to success stories of mothers who found a place behind a McDonald's counter—women who, according to the politicians, felt the enormous pride that comes with earning a minimum wage income and teaching your children to survive almost exclusively on dried noodles heated in a microwave. But when it came to sheer creativity, all the congressmen in the world were no match for Diane Lansford's ability to eke out a living while never crossing paths with a timecard.

Jimmy dug up and read through the TANF papers his mother brought home and threw in the trash. Reading the fine print, Jimmy understood he and Kelly were on a ticking clock. That was why, with few exceptions, Jimmy saved nearly every penny he earned.

He did not buy a car.

He did not save for college.

He did not tell his mother where he kept his money, despite her incessant, nagging requests to borrow just a few dollars.

"Can I borrow some money, please, baby?" Diane would ask, squeezing her breasts together and leaning toward Jimmy, as though he were a part-time welder with an uncashed $300 scratchers ticket in his pocket and not her own son. "I promise I'll pay you back."

Jimmy played this game before. He knew how his money would get used. Every dollar his mother could get her hands on went straight into a glass pipe.

"No, mom. Don't ask again," he said, keeping his eyes off her toxic leopard print.

Once rejected, she lost the flirty act and became the Diane he knew.

"Fucking ingrate," she would say.

TANF, food stamps, and Section 8 vouchers covered their rent, utilities, and what little food they kept in the house—but anything else was a luxury.

Jimmy tried to make do. His growing stardom in cross-country meant no one mocked his cheap running shoes. They were all he could afford—until one day he came home to a new pair of Nikes so clean and new they hurt to look at.

"Detective Carlisle dropped them off," Kelly said, her smile as bright as the new shoes sitting near his pillow. "Said he read about you in the paper and thought you might need them."

It was true; there was a story about Jimmy in the local paper, complete with a black-and-white photo of him holding a small trophy. He asked Brian if he could keep the trophy at his house. Jimmy was afraid Diane would believe it was real gold and attempt to pawn it or trade it for drugs. Brian said yes, though the trophy wasn't kept in his best friend's closet.

Brian's mom placed it on their mantle, right next to Brian's honor roll plaques and DECA trophy.

Jimmy was pretty sure it wasn't the last trophy he would hide from his mother. The first time he ran a mile in freshman PE, Jimmy discovered the lump in his throat—the lump threatening to escape as he looked at his new shoes—could be pushed down and out the bottom of his feet. When that happened, not even memories could catch him.

What their various forms of government assistance wouldn't pay for was the meth and Milwaukee's Best his mother consumed on a regular basis. He learned, a few months after they moved to their new home, how his mother earned her crystal money.

Jimmy was spending the night at Brian's house when Brian's mom knocked on her son's bedroom door. While the dairy was outside of town, it was part of the same school district Jimmy and Kelly always attended. Moving back to town didn't mean changing schools. Not having to change schools—even though it meant attending class with people who knew what a freakshow his family was—and being closer to Brian were two bright spots in an awful year.

It was past 11:00 PM when Brian's mom knocked on the door. Julie

Lucido didn't walk around with exposed cleavage, dyed blonde hair, and jeans so tight you could see geometry normally reserved for doctors and husbands. Julie wore flannel pajamas, was thick in her middle section, worked as an accountant, knew how to make homemade chocolate chip cookies, and wasn't shy about telling Brian how much she loved him. As best as Jimmy could tell, her favorite sentence was, "I love you, Bri."

After his sister, Brian's mom was the most beautiful woman Jimmy knew. Even in her flannel pajamas.

"Jimmy, Kelly's on the phone for you," Julie said from the doorway.

He had been lying on the floor, playing with Brian's old Gameboy. Jimmy secretly hoped Brian's new PlayStation meant he would get the Gameboy, just like the time Brian let him take the Walkman. Unlike the Walkman, if Brian gave him the Gameboy, Jimmy would be careful not to smash it.

Jimmy stood up and took the phone. Julie ruffled his hair, like she always did.

"Hey, Kelly. Everything okay?"

"I think someone is in our backyard. Inside mom's car," she said, her voice cracking and fading like a radio losing its signal. "I can see someone out there, and it isn't her."

"You sure? Where is mom?"

"I have no idea. Jimmy, I looked for her before I called you."

"What do you mean someone is in the car?"

In the middle of their overgrown backyard sat Diane's Pontiac Firebird, the passenger side window a spiderweb of broken glass, the bird on the hood long faded. The house had a driveway, but their mother could drunkenly weave the car down the alley and into their backyard without hitting the mailbox and coming face to face with a stack of past-due bills.

"I can see people in the car, and it's moving. I don't want to be here alone," Kelly said.

"Okay. I'm coming home. Lock the doors, and don't open them for anyone."

"Even mom?"

"Yes, even mom."

Especially mom, he wanted to say.

"Kay."

"Look under my bed. That's where I keep my weight plates. Get the ten-pound one."

"Kay."

"And where do you aim if someone breaks in? What did I tell you to do?"

"Hit them across the nose. With the weight plate. Let my wrists do the work."

"I'll be there as fast as I can."

"Kay."

"Kelly, lock all the doors. And do not let anyone in that isn't me."

"Kay."

"Bye."

"Jimmy?" Kelly asked before hanging up.

"Yeah?"

"Please hurry," she said. He caught the first forty percent of a sob before she hung up the phone. Jimmy imagined his little sister there, alone in the kitchen, as she placed the handset on the same rotary phone they had back on the farm into its cradle.

He pressed the off button on the Lucidos' cordless, and Julie immediately asked, "Is everything okay?"

Jimmy's best friend and his best friend's mom both looked at him, their shared facial structure showing equal parts pity, compassion, and genuine concern.

"I don't know. I gotta go home. Kelly needs me."

"Do you need me to call the police?" Julie asked, knowing what the answer would be. They had different versions of this same conversation on multiple occasions.

He knew he should call the police, knew he could even call Detective Carlisle directly and avoid the fiasco of their patchy front yard being illuminated by flashing reds and blues. While he could do that, he was pretty sure the person in the Firebird was his mother. She was probably banging away on the dash and the steering wheel, angry her car wouldn't start. Again.

"No, I think everything is okay. I just need to get home."

"I'll start the car. Meet me outside, I'll pack your stuff up and bring it to you tomorrow," Julie said. The path from Brian's middle-class street to Jimmy's Section 8 home was long, winding, and marked with unnecessary obstacles. But if he ran, he could cut through yards, ignore stoplights, and do whatever it took to get to his sister as fast he could.

"I'll run."

Julie recoiled like Jimmy slapped her.

"Jimmy Lansford, you will not."

She didn't have to say Jimmy would run right through the worst part of town. Though Garrity was relatively small, the drug trade was run by men who maintained market share in neighborhoods like Jimmy's by using extreme violence.

"Ms. Lucido—"

"Jimmy, you know you can call me Julie."

"Julie, I can get there faster by running."

"Jimmy—"

Julie's objections fell on deaf ears. Jimmy laced up the Nikes Carlisle bought him and was out Brian's door before she could stop him. Within a few seconds he was running down the smooth concrete path splitting the Lucidos' manicured lawn.

Jimmy ran past the other upper-middle-class homes until they slowly became lower- middle-class, Toyotas and the occasional Lexus replaced by late-model Chevrolet Blazers. Decent homes then morphed into 24-hour gas stations and liquor stores and smoke shops, where customers didn't even bother to open their car doors before twisting open one of the six Mickey's malt liquor grenades they just purchased. He ran until the liquor stores and smoke shops faded into apartment buildings and trailer parks, dwellings that would one day be extracted from the ground like rotted teeth and blown all the way to Missouri by an Oklahoma tornado. The farther he ran, the less reliable lighting he had, and his silhouette passed in and out of the few remaining streetlights; one second Jimmy was in the spotlight, the next he was swallowed by the night.

As he ran, Jimmy ignored late-night catcalls from drunks who had the good sense to have their Mickey's already on hand. Men who peaked four years after they left their mother's womb sat on their front porches mocking a boy who knew how and when to run.

Jimmy reached their house and used the key to open the front door. He found Kelly, wide-eyed and sitting on their couch, a weight plate in her hands, just like Jimmy taught her. She wore one of his cross-country shirts and pajama pants, her brown hair up in a ponytail.

Kelly had changed in the year since their father died. Regular brushes with terror made his sister look and sound more and more like a little girl. Jimmy hoped it was temporary. He needed her hard edges. He would always remember his father's fist looming above his face, knuckles white, as Kelly leapt on Ronnie's back and bit into the stinking stubble-flecked flesh of their father's neck.

Jimmy went in their kitchen and looked out the window. Kelly was right; there were people inside the Firebird. The car rocked from side to side, the rusty shocks emitting soft, squeaky moans.

"Hand me that," he said, pointing to the weight plate in Kelly's hands.

Kelly walked over and gave Jimmy the weight plate.

"Same thing," he said. "Don't let anyone in unless it's me. Not even mom."

"Kay," she said.

Jimmy opened their backdoor and stepped into a backyard choked with cigarette butts and empty brown bags stained dark with Tater tot grease. He accidently kicked a beer can. Milwaukee's Best sloshed around the bottom. A little beer spilled on the front of his shoes. Of all his material possessions, his Nikes were most important to him. The first night he owned them he fell asleep with his face buried in a shoe, smelling first-hand footwear for the first time in his life.

"Fuck," he whispered, looking down at the beer stain on the toe of his Nike.

The Firebird continued rocking. Jimmy kept the weight plate cocked above his head, ready to bring the iron down hard on anyone who might jump out and rush him.

The only light in the backyard came from the weak glow of their kitchen window. The spot where the backyard faded into a dirt alley was almost pitch black. Whatever was happening in the Firebird was happening on the passenger side of the vehicle, the side obscured by the web of cracks in the glass. Jimmy moved slowly through the tall grass until he could see into the car.

In the passenger seat sat a man with long salt-and-pepper hair and a short goatee, his tattooed arms bulging from his sleeveless shirt. A lit cigarette dangled from his mouth, the ash ready to fall at any moment. Facing the man, in his lap, was his mother. She didn't have her shirt or pants on, and her eyes were closed. On the driver's seat there were several crumpled bills, some fives and tens—but mostly ones—a can of Milwaukee's Best, a cloudy pipe, and a bag of white rocks.

Just like earlier in the night, Jimmy ran. Back through the backyard, up the stairs, onto the porch, and through the backdoor. Kelly was waiting on the couch for him holding another weight plate, ready to let her wrists do the work.

"Come with me," Jimmy said.

"Who's out there?" Kelly asked.

"You're going to help me. I need to practice. I need to run," Jimmy said, leading Kelly back to their shared bedroom.

"Right now?"

"Yes, right now," Jimmy said, looking back toward the kitchen. Outside, the Firebird still rocked, still moved side to side. Kelly grabbed her brother's hand, their fingers locking together. They didn't hold hands like lovers at a matinee. They white-knuckle gripped each other the way the condemned do when they are marched toward their end.

"Jimmy, I don't—"

"Kelly, please. Please run with me."

Kelly stood on her tiptoes, peering back down the hallway.

"Who was out there?"

"Mom."

"Mom? What's she doing? Why are we running from mom?"

"Please, Kelly. We need to get out of here."

She sighed and looked at the door to their backyard.

"Okay," she said, "but mom borrowed my shoes."

Jimmy spit on his hands, rubbed them together, and used them to wipe the slight yellow of the beer from the toe of his right Nike.

"You'll wear these. It will be okay."

"Jimmy! I can't wear your shoes. They're huge on me."

Jimmy stood up and placed his hands on his sister's shoulders.

"Listen to me," he said. "These shoes are magic. Carlisle knew that. That's why he bought them."

Kelly squeezed his hand tighter and looked up at her brother "You don't need magic shoes. You're fast as shit, Jimmy. Everyone knows that."

"Exactly. But if you wear magic shoes, you'll be fast as shit too."

Kelly didn't believe in magic—she knew they couldn't afford a hat, let alone a rabbit—but she believed in her brother. Fiercely.

"Kay," she said.

Though Jimmy hadn't laced Kelly up in years, that night he bent down and put his prized possessions on his sister's feet. Once he finished with Kelly, Jimmy laced up his old sneakers, kept in a box under his bed just in case his mother pawned his Nikes.

"Let's go," he said, grabbing Kelly's hand.

Once out the door Jimmy started running, moderating his pace so he didn't get ahead of Kelly. His sister wasn't a good runner to begin with, and the oversized shoes weren't helping. The Nikes flopped on pitted sidewalks as they crossed streets named for presidents. Washington, Jefferson, and Monroe. Virginia's finest, littered with empty Joe Camel soft packs and Schlitz Malt Liquor tallboys.

"Jimmy, I can't keep up," Kelly said. The expression his sister made when she was trying not to cry was something Jimmy was familiar with. The site of her face as it crumpled and re-inflated and then crumpled again broke his heart. He would rather watch his mother eat a hundred pounds of crystal meth than see that look pass over his sister's face.

They stood under a broken streetlight. Unlike Brian's well-lit neighborhood, when the sun went down in Jimmy's part of town, darkness was all-consuming.

"It's okay, Kelly. We'll just walk fast. It's okay, Kelly. It's okay. It's okay."

"No, Jimmy. I can't do it. Let's go home," she said, grabbing his hand and looking him in the eye. "It's just mom."

Just mom? He thought. Like when he and Brian would hear footsteps upstairs, and Brian would see the panicked look in his best friend's eyes and say, "Don't worry, it's just my mom doing laundry"—or like when he and Kelly would hear a terrible commotion in their kitchen, and Jimmy would check to see if everything was okay, only to find Diane in her godawful (and godawfully short) Van Halen shirt, hunting a chemically hallucinated rat with a plastic spork from KFC, and Jimmy would come back to their room and say, "Don't worry, it's just mom"?

"Just mom": in a normal house, two words so mundane and innocuous no one even noticed when they were said.

"Kelly, mom—"

"Jimmy, sometimes I sound like a little kid. I know that. But I'm not stupid. I know what she's doing out there."

Jimmy pulled his sister close, his nostrils filling with the smell of her citrus shampoo. Dogs barked as the wind picked up, the litter lining Monroe Street becoming Dust Bowl tumbleweeds without bowls, or even dust.

"Jimmy, it's okay. It's just mom. She won't hurt us."

Mom has already hurt us, he wanted to say. Dad too. They fucked everything up before we even got here, and never bothered to fix it once we arrived. Our father put us in the newspaper way before my legs ever did, and our mother is a backyard whore. They hurt us, Kelly. And all they do is keep hurting us.

Maybe Kelly held out hope that there might be something worthwhile inside of their mother. Despite their many, many flaws, Diane and Ronnie Lansford managed to raise two exceptional children. Perhaps that objective, indisputable fact was the source of Kelly's faith in their mother. Or maybe she didn't think that. Maybe Kelly knew who and what their mother was and just didn't see the point in running through the darkness toward nothing.

Their father was an only child, his parents having died while driving home drunk from a bar. Their mother's family was no better off than they were and would not be thrilled about the idea of sharing their own TANF money and food stamps with a teenage niece and nephew. They had nowhere to go, so instead of running toward the unknown, Kelly decided to turn around and head back toward what she knew: their mother, and a house where plunging your nose into the dark recesses of a Goodwill couch constituted getting a breath of fresh air.

Jimmy decided not to fight her. He couldn't ask Brian's family to take him and Kelly in, though he was sure Brian's mom would have beds made and warm chocolate chip cookies ready and waiting, even at this hour. But while he could take his friend's electronic hand-me-downs, he wouldn't take his pity.

The only other responsible person they really knew in town was Detective Carlisle, and Jimmy couldn't ask him to take him and his sister in—plus, Jimmy assumed Carlisle's involvement, no matter how well intentioned, always came with the inherent risk of his biggest fear: he and Kelly separated and in foster care.

When it came to Carlisle, Jimmy's assumption was incorrect. Even though he was far too young to be their father, if given half a chance Carlisle would become Jimmy and Kelly's legal guardian in a heartbeat. The last thing he would do is involve the Department of Child Services, which was the same branch of government that thought Jimmy and Kelly were safe under the care of Diane Lansford.

Rather than run toward Brian's house or go to a payphone and dial Mike Carlisle's number, Jimmy and Kelly turned around and walked home. In their backyard, a man with a sleeveless shirt and thick tattooed arms finished smoking out his mother before leaving the wadded-up money on the driver's seat and walking toward the truck he parked in the alley.

Alone and sweaty, the man's semen running from her vagina onto the Firebird's sun-cracked vinyl, Diane laid the passenger seat back. She gazed at a starless Oklahoma night through the Firebird's T-tops.

Though there was nothing to see, Diane heard the roar of an imaginary black helicopter settling just above her—the state coming to take her children away.

Over her dead fucking body, she thought.

Just try it.

Her children were hers, and she would do with them what she pleased. As she looked through the Firebird's roof, her lips slowly pulled back from her teeth. Her nose scrunched up, her hands curled into claws. She let out a cry that sounded to the neighborhood dogs like one of their own, and they barked back in response.

Diane didn't hear them. She dug her fingernails into her thighs, scratching and picking until they were raw and red. She felt the pressure of the whirring rotors in her mind as they beat down on the Firebird, pinning her against the seat.

This black helicopter sent by that cop her kids were getting chummy with was not going to take Jimmy and Kelly.

If Jimmy's observer traveled back in time to this night in 1998 and stood in the spot where the backyard faded into the alley, it would see a naked woman, her eyes bottomless black pupils, her teeth bared as she screamed at a sky full of nothing.

If it crawled into the dark and polluted corners of Diane's mind and looked through the glass T-tops, it would see an obsidian helicopter just inches above the car's roof. It would hear the apocalyptic THUMP-THUMP-THUMP of the world's loudest rotors.

The observer would feel the icy cold rush of crystal meth race through its body, its toes growing cold as its brain overheated.

Despite the terror of the moment, it would want more.

And more.

And more.

And more.

It would fear the helicopter, yet as soon as the crystal ran its course, it would do anything—even sell its body—to see the helicopter again. This was one reason the observer would never visit this home, never travel back in time to 1998.

Some things, the observer knew, were much scarier than faded handprints in an empty hotel room.

Inside the house, Jimmy tucked Kelly in. He left his magic Nikes on her feet. After kissing her forehead, Jimmy reached beneath his bed, looking for the Walkman he purchased to replace the one destroyed at the farmhouse. Like the beginner's weight set he bought, the Walkman justified dipping into the money he saved from his job at Derry's. Though he splurged on the Walkman, he couldn't justify a Discman, and the Lansford siblings still used tapes, rather than CDs.

But at least they had music.

Outside Jimmy heard his mother scream. He put the headphones over Kelly's ears. He turned on Cyndi Lauper and lay in bed as his sister dozed off to her favorite song. Jimmy stayed awake, his eyes wide open, keeping watch over the person he loved most, waiting for another scream. Hours later, as he slept, Jimmy unconsciously bared his canines at the sound of Diane Lansford re-entering their home.

CHAPTER NINE

2019

Jimmy's home office was decorated with pictures of Jill, Jonathan, and Jessica, trophies and ribbons from his college cross-country days, and his framed MBA. No remnant of the boy Jimmy Lansford was or the family he came from—aside from the framed picture of Kelly on their kitchen counter—was allowed in his home. "Leave no trace of childhood Jimmy" was his rule, but it was a rule he was about to break.

The week before, Jimmy Googled "Mike Carlisle Garrity Oklahoma" and learned his old friend became chief of Garrity's police department in 2011. That didn't surprise Jimmy. What did surprise him was that he actually copied and pasted Carlisle's email address into his Gmail account. He didn't think he would go through with it, until he hit Ctrl V on his keyboard.

Carlisle responded almost instantly, emailing Jimmy back less than an hour later. Now Jimmy waited for the Skype connection to go through, his stomach roiled by nostalgia and nausea.

"Oh my God," Jimmy said.

The face of a man who was once the closest thing Jimmy had to a father figure appeared onscreen. It had been eighteen years since they last saw each other.

"My man," Carlisle said. "Eighteen years."

"Eighteen years," Jimmy said.

The entire span of one complete childhood, Jimmy thought.

"How's that wife of yours doing? Your kids?" Carlisle asked.

"Good, good. They're all healthy. Growing up fast, man. I'm lucky."

"What do you do, Jimmy?"

Carlisle remembered all their conversations about Jimmy's education and career.

"I'm a futures trader—mostly milk, some pork belly," Jimmy said.

"You can do that from Phoenix?"

Jimmy laughed, one of the few good laughs he'd had in weeks.

"It's 2019," Jimmy said. "You can trade milk futures from anywhere. You just have to have a computer and read a whole lot about what's going on in the rest of the world, and how it will or won't affect milk prices three months from now. Boring stuff, to most people—but I like it. What about you? Do you and Claudia have any kids?"

"Three. Getting bigger every day."

Carlisle thought of Jimmy and Kelly every time he looked at one of his babies for the first time. He understood why, for Jimmy, leaving home meant leaving behind all things Oklahoma. There were no hard feelings. Carlisle told Jimmy to leave and never look back.

"How old are you now?" Jimmy asked.

"Fifty! Can you believe it?"

"Fifty? Wow. You look great."

"Well, you know what they say," Carlisle said. "Black don't crack."

Carlisle laughed and stroked a face that looked almost as youthful as the day they first met. Jimmy could not say the same about his own aging, and Carlisle respected him enough to not offer a false compliment in return.

"So," Carlisle said, "I wasn't expecting to get an email from you. Hadn't heard from you in ages."

"It's about my father. Do you remember that day?"

A man with a knife buried handle-deep in his eye socket. A woman under a bathroom sink holding a lighter to a packed glass bulb. Two brave children holding each other, one staring wide-eyed at his father's dead body. A detective wondering if the knife might be a blessing, trying to push away the thought the real blessed event would have been two dead Lansford parents staring through a hole in a barn roof.

"Of course I remember that day."

Outside of Jill and his kids, Jimmy assumed he occupied little space in the minds and hearts of others. He didn't need a psychiatrist to tell him why, either. He could go Dr. Phil on himself just fine. Like all children, he once believed he was the center of his parents' universe. But over the years, he was reminded time and time again that he and Kelly were unfortunate obstacles—at best. It took him a while, but by the time he was five, Diane and Ronnie conditioned Jimmy to expect no compassion from others.

"I'm sorry. I know. I know me and Kelly were important to you. Do you know I still have those first Nikes you got me?"

"Really?! Shoot, that's amazing. You could run, my man. You could run."

"Those shoes made all the difference in the world. You know that, right?"

Carlisle smiled. He knew that wasn't the truth. When Jimmy was in high school, he could have worn Kleenex boxes on his feet and won medals. The shoes weren't bought to make him run faster. The shoes were a monument to love and belief, carved by a Nike swoosh.

"Thank you, Jimmy. That means a lot to me. Now, ask me what you want to ask me."

"My father."

"Yes?"

"I've just never asked...never said this out loud...my father—"

"Let me stop you right there. I think I know what you're going to ask."

Jimmy thought Carlisle couldn't possibly know the question he would ask.

"There were legitimate questions. Do you know how rare it is for someone to take their own life the way your father did?"

"It's...rare."

"Yeah, really rare. I still Google it every now and again, wondering if anyone else has decided to go out that way. They haven't."

"I know. I Google it, too."

"Then I know what you're asking. It's the same question we had, and for years I thought she killed him. But I've believed, ever since your mother passed, that she didn't kill your father. She was a horrible...she caused an incredible amount of pain. But, she did not kill your father. That I'm sure of."

"My mother?"

"Diane was a lot of things. She was a monster. A monster. She didn't kill your father, though."

The thought hadn't occurred to him, not once in the twenty-two years since his father died. Perhaps he was naïve; perhaps he didn't want to think the woman who carried him in her womb could be a killer.

"How do you know?" Jimmy asked.

"Because your mother was a drunk and an addict and a loudmouth. I'm sorry, I just, what she did to you kids, your—"

"It's okay. You don't need to feel bad. Say what you have to say."

"She was a loudmouth, and half the people she got drugs from were on our payroll. They were informants. Or, snitches, if you prefer. Even that guy Crowder she dated was a snitch. If she mentioned killing your father even once, we would have heard about it. Someone would cut a deal and give her up to shake a charge. No honor among thieves. Or methheads."

"Why would she admit it? And why would she admit it to another addict?"

Carlisle leaned back in his chair and drummed his fingers on his desk. He knew Jimmy had seen the worst the world can offer, but the inner workings of a small-town drug trade were likely lost on a milk futures trader.

"You don't think someone ever shorted her in all those years of buying crystal? You know they did. More than once. If she killed your father, the first words out of her mouth would have been, 'I'll kill you, you blankety-blankety blank mf'er. I've done it before.' That didn't happen, not once. I don't think your mother is innocent because she's a good person. She was a bad person. But at some point, if she had killed him, she would have used it to threaten someone. We have people who make up murders all the time for intimidation. 'Don't f with me, I put a knife in so-and-so.' That sort of thing. If she were sober, I would think she just knew how to keep her mouth shut, and maybe she did kill him. But she was never sober."

Jimmy looked at a picture on his desk of the family he and Jill pulled from their shared hat, a magic trick that saved one life and created two others. Carlisle couldn't see what Jimmy was looking at but had a good idea who he was thinking about.

"You didn't leave, Jimmy. You moved away. For something better. You had to."

The lump in Jimmy's throat had been back for a while, ever since he first started spontaneously weeping. That night, looking at Carlisle, the lump was more swollen than ever. But he would not cry in front of this man who bought him his first real pair of running shoes.

Jimmy braced himself to say what he only thought, what he was sure Carlisle would laugh at.

"I don't think my father was murdered."

There was a pause, and then Jimmy asked Carlisle the question he wanted to ask.

"What if my father was possessed?"

Carlisle sat at his desk not moving or speaking long enough for Jimmy to think Skype was frozen.

"Hold on," Carlisle said. He stood from his desk and left the screen. Jimmy heard a door close, and moments later Carlisle re-entered the Skype frame and sat back down in his chair. It was clear Carlisle's graceful aging wasn't limited to his face. He was still fit. He doubted the chief chased suspects down a dark alley, but Carlisle would still be able to hold his own.

"Possessed? You mean, by the devil?"

Carlisle did not snicker or smile. He took Jimmy seriously.

"Yeah. Possessed. I don't know if it was the devil...but possessed by something. I—I know how it sounds," Jimmy said.

"Jimmy. Don't...don't worry about how it sounds."

"I know it sounds crazy."

"Jimmy, if there were ever two people who were possessed by the devil, it was your parents."

The chief gave Jimmy a stern look—the same stern look he used when he stopped joking around and gave his children Serious Life Advice.

"But either way they're long gone. You need to live your life. Embrace those babies of yours before they move away and go to college. Make a few friends. Heck, maybe I'll come see you out in Phoenix and we'll go watch a Diamondbacks game."

"Can you be sure?"

"You know, when I was young, a young cop, I thought supernatural evil was a possible explanation for things I saw. A year before I met you and Kelly, I went out on a call on a domestic. The guy wasn't just a wife beater. He also adopted cats from the local shelter. The shelter folks loved him. You know what he did with those cats? He would take them home and cut chunks out of them—not enough to kill the cat, just enough to hurt it. He would cauterize the wound and bandage it. If the cat lived, he would do it again. He wanted to see how much a living thing could take before it died—when its will to live, its will to endure, just gave out. Oh, and the chunks he would cut out? He fed those to other cats. Jimmy, sometimes I wish there was an explanation as simple as the devil."

"You don't think it's even a possibility?"

"Jimmy…I think some people are born bad, some people are raised bad, and some people grow to be bad. No offense, Jimmy, but I think your parents were born bad and were raised bad, and then put a whole bunch of crap in their bodies that made what was already bad even worse. That's a big reason why you and Kelly stuck with me, why I cared—why I care so much about both of you. Still. Even now. So, no, I don't think your parents—your dad—was possessed. I don't…I don't like cussing like this, but your dad was a mean fuck-up who married a mean fuck-up and together they fucked each other up even worse. But…what do you think?"

Jimmy stared at a man whose opinion he respected more than any man he ever knew, including and especially Ronnie Lansford.

"I—partly it's the method. My father didn't seem like he was strong enough, and I've read—"

"I hear you. Possession supposedly gives people physical capabilities they don't have."

"Yeah, how—"

"We've all seen *The Exorcist*, Jimmy. Crystal meth also makes people think they're Superman. Sometimes they take the crazy out on their own bodies."

"Okay. Well, there's that. But his suicide note. Did you read his note?"

"There's something inside me? Right? All caps? Hard to forget that."

Carlisle remembered removing the note from Kelly's hands, the blood on her small hands drying to a crunchy brown.

"Yes. That, and there was always just a—just a feeling. In my house. In my family."

"I won't argue about that. As soon as I stepped foot on the dairy, I felt the need to vomit," Carlisle said, looking down and then back up at the screen. "I remember…I walked into your bathroom and puked in the sink. I just lost it. Everywhere."

"What?"

"Yeah. I remember feeling nauseous and puking up my breakfast in your sink. I wiped a little off the mirror. It was, at least as far as I remember, the only time I ever vomited on scene. I was embarrassed. But Jimmy, none of this is new information. You've had his suicide note for a long time. Why now? Why look me up to go over stuff we've both known for so long?"

Jimmy couldn't avoid it.

"Because it's—something is happening in my house. I don't understand—I think—"

Carlisle raised his hand. Were they not separated by a thousand miles and two decades, the hand would lie on Jimmy's chest rather than filling a screen.

"Jimmy, I'm not going to ask you to justify your reason for getting ahold of me, or for wondering if your father was possessed. But I want to tell you something, and I want you to listen."

"Okay."

"If the devil is real, then it stands to reason there is his opposite, right?"

"Yeah. I mean, right. That makes sense. But—"

"You had it bad growing up. The worst I've seen in Garrity, and things can be pretty bad here. Your sister experienced even worse. Your father killed himself, and sometimes I thought that was best, before he could hurt you or Kelly. That's how bad it was. Your mom was a dope fiend, and a mean dope fiend at that."

"We don't need to recap everything," Jimmy said, trying to sound like he was joking. It did not work.

"Point being, anyone can comb through their past, looking for the devil. Anyone. Even those of us with a...a more normal life. Crap. I don't mean 'normal.' I'm sorry, I—"

"It's okay. I know what you mean."

"Yeah, well, I apologize. Sometimes I have a big mouth. Point is, since you moved away, look at your life. I've kept an eye on you. I don't have a Facebook page myself, but I can see yours, and you've got a beautiful family. Beautiful wife. Beautiful kids—and, my goodness, your little girl looks a lot like her Aunt Kelly. Spitting image."

"She does," Jimmy said. Jessica and Kelly could be mistaken for twins, if they were the same age.

"Maybe evil has touched your life. Maybe. Maybe it was just bad luck. Most definitely bad parenting. But I do know, without a doubt, that good has made itself part of your life. Look at your profile pic, Jimmy. Someone is looking after you, and it isn't the devil. You like Springsteen?"

"What?"

"Do you like Bruce Springsteen?" Carlisle asked.

"Do *you* like Bruce Springsteen? I mean—"

Carlisle laughed his good laugh.

"You think black people don't like Springsteen?"

"No, it's just—"

Carlisle laughed again.

"It's okay, Jimmy. I'm joking. Springsteen has a line in one of his songs that says for too long he kept his good eye to the dark, and his blind eye to the sun. You know what that means?"

"I think I get it."

"Well, Jimmy, if you think you're possessed, or haunted, or whatever, I won't doubt you, and I won't make you feel small because of it—provided we keep up with these calls. Look, even I know your kids should be somewhere around the age you and Kelly were when your father died. It's a hard time for you, I get that, and I'm here for you—but please, please keep your good eye to the sun. Please."

Jimmy knew it was good advice. It was also advice that was hard to follow when it felt like you floated out of a storage unit and into space.

It was time to tell Carlisle goodbye. Jimmy was in the upstairs office, and Jill or one of the kids would soon knock on the door and tell him dinner was getting cold. He couldn't let them overhear a conversation about possession. Before he went, though, needed to ask Carlisle one more question.

"Can I ask you something, one more thing before we go?"

"Sure. Ask away. And if you're inviting Claudia and me over for Thanksgiving, know the answer is yes. We'll come. All the way to Phoenix."

Jimmy smiled, remembering a pile of homemade mashed potatoes Claudia made that were still the best thing—outside of Jill's cooking—he ever tasted.

"One night I came home from a sleepover. Kelly was scared and asked me to come home. When I got home our mother was outside with Crowder in that Firebird that was in our backyard. Back then I didn't know it was Crowder. I hadn't met him yet. She was doing it for drugs and a little money, but mostly drugs. I got Kelly and we took off running, and I thought about calling you, but—"

"You weren't sure I would answer?"

"No. I knew you would answer the phone. I wanted to ask you if we could come over and—"

"Jimmy, I would have taken you and Kelly in a heartbeat. That night, and every night after. Finding you two, and what you've become, Jimmy, it...it made what I've spent my life doing worth it. All the crap I've seen—you two were just worth it. I loved—I still love you. Both of you. And, I understand why you left all this behind—heck, I helped you do it—but Jimmy, I miss you. I miss Kelly. I think about you two a lot, and I just—I miss you."

Jimmy did his best to keep the tears inside, especially when his kids might see. Emotional stability was something he prioritized. Growing up, tears weren't a sign of vulnerability, sorrow, or joy. They were precursors to or the direct result of sudden violence. But hearing Carlisle tell him he loved him, and his sister, was too much. Tears ran down his cheeks and into his open shirt collar, coming to rest in the hard lines of his runner's belly.

"Why?" he asked, his voice cracking.

"Why do I love you guys?"

"Yeah."

"Because, Jimmy. That's what big brothers do."

Jimmy let out a bark, a suppressed cry caged at the base of his throat for a long, long time. He placed his fist against the screen. Carlisle did the same.

They said their goodbyes, their fists leaving the screen long after the Skype connection ended. Both hoped this wasn't the last time they would talk. Carlisle told Jimmy not to be a stranger and said again that he loved him. Other than his son, Jimmy had never said those words to another man. It felt good to tell Carlisle he loved him, too.

Jimmy left his home office, washing his face and hands in the same bathroom Jill had found him in during Jessica's birthday party. That night there was no smudge in the mirror, no spontaneous vomiting, no presence standing with him—just three people yelling from the dining room that dinner was indeed getting colder.

Though Jimmy would suspect the devil's work throughout his home in the coming days, the visit with Carlisle was good, and needed.

As visits with big brothers usually are.

CHAPTER TEN

1999

Jimmy planned to run until he and Kelly lived in a small apartment that smelled like Hot Pockets and Lysol, a clean drywall box somewhere in Norman or Stillwater. He didn't care if he became an Oklahoma Sooner or an Oklahoma State Cowboy.

He just wanted out of Garrity and as far away from Diane as he could imagine.

Kelly would get the apartment's only bedroom. Jimmy would crash on a cheap Walmart futon purchased with his milkshake savings. He would work after school and on the weekends, waiting tables, mowing lawns, scratching by. Kelly would have to work, too, after school at McDonald's, a daycare, or even babysitting. Money would be tight, and life would be hard, but it wouldn't matter.

Life was already hard.

They would never hear the Firebird rocking back and forth in their backyard. They would never have to defend themselves with weight plates. They would never drink rust-colored water from chipped glasses.

In the meantime, they would endure.

Sometimes, when Diane returned from her occasional disappearances, Jimmy took the keys to the Firebird. Escape had a price, and for Jimmy that price was paid when he and Kelly sat on stained vinyl seats that doubled as Diane's home office. Diane signed the permission slip for Jimmy to take driver's ed at school—she might need cigarettes, and he was almost eighteen—and Carlisle taught him to drive using the lieutenant's old Toyota

Camry.

They would drive to 7-Eleven, and Jimmy would buy banana Slurpees and a small package of Twizzlers. They would bite both ends off their licorice, using the candy for straws as the Firebird's one working headlight probed better neighborhoods, like low-rent burglars shining their flashlight in someone else's home.

"I want that one," Kelly once said, pointing to a huge house in the nicest part of town with an entrance more like a hotel than a home. Jimmy had never stayed in a hotel, but when he grew up he promised himself if he did, he would gorge himself on as much room service as one man could eat.

"Why that one?" Jimmy asked.

"Because it looks like it has a pool," Kelly said.

"A pool?" Jimmy could only imagine. He and Kelly had never been to a swimming pool, and there is no ocean in Oklahoma. Neither knew how to swim.

They would return home after their drives, where they would usually find their mother passed out on the couch, or in her room, a sixer of Milwaukee's Best having dulled her rage.

Sometimes Jimmy would dip into his savings and buy himself and Kelly a tube of premade chocolate chip cookie dough, and the two would cook half the dough and eat the other half raw.

More than anything, Jimmy learned even a nightmare can become routine. His high school life was a day-in, day-out grind of events no child should experience, words no child should hear. But as bad as the monotony could be, disruption to the monotony was even worse.

One such disruption occurred when their mother began dating Roger, the man Jimmy had seen with her in the Firebird.

Dating would be a charitable word to describe the interaction between Diane Lansford and Roger Crowder. As far as Jimmy could tell, the relationship consisted of Roger eating all the food in their house, giving his mother her fix, calling Jimmy a pussy, and leering at Kelly. He could tolerate the first three, but after weeks of Roger living on their couch and staring at Kelly every time she was around, Jimmy could no longer take it. The last straw came when Crowder tried to explain away walking in on Kelly while she showered as an accident.

The day Roger walked in on Kelly, Jimmy dialed the pager number Mike

Carlisle gave him.

Kelly was gone, staying after school at art club. The Lansford children joined every possible club and afterschool activity they could, the school knowing ahead of time they needed to waive any fee. Diane was gone, working one of the downtown bars for more cash. Roger could supply her drugs, but she still needed to earn money. He made that clear. Roger himself was sitting on their couch in a too-small tank top, eating generic Rice Krispies by the handful, straight from the box.

Within seconds the phone rang, and Jimmy picked it up immediately.

"Jimmy?" Carlisle asked.

"It's me."

"My man. Is everything okay?"

"Yeah," Jimmy said, watching Crowder on the couch. His mother's boyfriend ate a bit of cereal he dug out of his exposed belly button. "I—hey, can I meet you later, if you have time? I have something I want to talk to you about. How about we meet at Derry's?"

"See you there in twenty," Carlisle said.

Jimmy went in his room, laced up his Nikes—which were now painfully tight, but still nicer than any other shoes he could afford—and ran to Derry's. When he arrived, Carlisle was waiting for him with a melting ice cream cone in each hand.

"My man," he said as Jimmy walked up and sat down.

"Hey," Jimmy said.

Carlisle handed him one of the ice cream cones.

"How's running?"

"Good," Jimmy said. "I came in second at regionals. That means I'm going to State."

"State! Jimmy, I'm proud of you."

If Jimmy became just a half-decent human being, Carlisle would be proud. But the boy he met the day he answered a call about a man stabbing himself in the eyeball was a lot more than just half-decent. Jimmy had become an academic and athletic star—and a father to his little sister.

"Thank you. These shoes still work. Still magic."

Carlisle saw the shoes were nearing the end of their useful life. Jimmy struggled to ask for anything, which is why he knew this visit was important.

"Tell me, Jimmy, what do you need?"

"My mom is dating a guy named Roger Crowder—"

"I know Roger Crowder."

As a police officer, Carlisle knew both Roger Crowder specifically and his kind generally. Roger was a low-level dealer and an informant to the police department—a snitch—and came from a breed who talked of loyalty, toughness, and manhood as though they knew the meaning of any of those words.

"He—Roger looks at my sister. All the time. He walked in on her while she was showering."

Carlisle was known among his colleagues for a steady hand and an ability to stay cool in any situation. Well, almost any situation.

An aspiring child molester was not one of those situations.

"Has he hurt you or your sister?" Carlisle asked, his fists clenched beneath the sun-faded plastic picnic table.

"No. Not yet. I won't let Kelly be alone with him."

"Okay. Let me have a talk with him. I can get this straightened out. Where's Kelly now?"

"Still at school. Art club."

"Is she safe?"

"Yeah, she's safe."

"Why don't I drop you off at school so you can meet her. Take this," Carlisle said, handing Jimmy a twenty-dollar bill, "and take her to the movies tonight."

"I have money. It's okay."

"Jimmy. Take the twenty, go see the movies, and come home. Take the bus. I know you like to run, but don't run through your part of town with your sister. Got it?"

"Got it."

That night, as Jimmy and Kelly watched a movie with Will Smith in a cowboy hat and ate Sour Patch Kids, Mike Carlisle parked three houses down from the Lansfords' house. He wore his civilian clothes, knowing pleated Gap khakis are the least dangerous mask a dangerous man can wear. He doubled down on the false harmlessness by driving his Toyota Camry, the pleated Gap khakis of cars.

He was sure Roger would leave to go get smokes and liquor, and an hour and a half after Carlisle parked his Camry on the darkened road, Roger

Crowder drunkenly stumbled out of the Lansford home and into a beat-up Chevy truck.

Carlisle started his car and followed for a block before pulling a siren out of his glovebox and placing it on the roof. Half a block of bobbing and weaving later, Crowder finally edged the Chevy toward the curb, nicking the concrete with a rusted-out wheel before coming to a stop.

Carlisle exited his vehicle and walked up to the driver's side of the truck. Crowder rolled down his window. Inside Carlisle could see the floor littered with empty beer cans. Good, Carlisle thought. Probable cause.

Just in case he needed an explanation for the higher-ups.

"Step out of the car," Carlisle said. "And turn off your headlights."

"What?" Crowder slurred, his gut tight against the bottom of the truck's steering wheel.

No gun on the seat, as far as he could tell—which was too bad. Before this conversation was over, he might need that for his explanation, too.

"I won't say it again. Step out of the car. Turn your lights off."

Carlisle pulled his flashlight, shining it into the truck's filthy cab. Crowder shielded his eyes. With the glare reduced, Crowder—even in his intoxicated state—recognized Carlisle and smiled a wet, slow smile. It amused him, this black cop who hid behind the authority of his badge. If it weren't for that badge, Crowder could kick the shit out of him. He was sure of it.

"I know...I know you. You're that BLACK cop," Crowder said, leaning back against the seat. He tried winking at Carlisle, but only managed a long two-eyed blink before asking a short one-word question.

"Remove yourself from the vehicle, Mr. Crowder," Carlisle said. "Or I will remove you."

Crowder opened his door and stood with a groan, his long hair and growing belly the direct opposite of Carlisle's buzzcut and hard muscles.

"Face me," Carlisle said.

Crowder ignored him, stretching his back like he was urinating as he looked at the front porch of a long-abandoned mobile home.

"You know, I grew up in this neighborhood," Crowder said. "It was a good place then. People worked. Kept their fuckin' mouth shut. Good people. Good fuckin' folks. Folks you could share a pool with."

"Look me in the eye, boy," Carlisle said, "Or I will make you look me in the eye."

"You can't talk to me that way," Crowder said, turning to face Carlisle, who was not surprised Crowder complied. That's what his kind was all about: big words and a deep desire for someone else to tell them what to do and how to think.

Crowder and Carlisle stood facing one another in the street, Crowder a foot or so away from the driver's door of his Chevy. The sound of a dog barking came from the trailer park behind Crowder. The dog's bark was followed by someone yelling, "Shut that fucking dog up!" which was followed by someone else yelling "You shut the fuck up!" which was, blissfully, followed by everyone shutting the fuck up. Even the dog.

Roger Crowder smiled, comfortable in his natural element.

During his senior year in high school, no one in Oklahoma swung a baseball bat as hard or as fast as Mike Carlisle. He used that swing to earn a bachelor's degree in criminal justice after four years in Norman.

Placing both hands on the flashlight, Carlisle looked down at his knuckles and wrists. They were older and thicker than they were back when his teammates would wear Hammer pants out to the Bluebonnet bar. That was so long ago, Carlisle thought. Time really did fly.

His technique would be sloppy.

He would have to compensate with force.

Carlisle stepped into his swing, and let his wrists do the rest—just like he was taught. Crowder's face exploded as what was left of the rotten bones jutting from his gums fell from his lips.

Carlisle knew another blow above the shoulders could kill the man. On the second swing Carlisle aimed to not just hurt Crowder but to do him and whatever little girl crossed his path next a favor. The head of the flashlight hit Crowder's crotch hard enough to momentarily lift him off the ground.

Crowder lay on the pavement, spitting blood and shards of teeth, clutching his destroyed genitals. Carlisle squatted down and waited for the bloodied man to return to a state where he could hear what Carlisle said. Crowder dry-heaved a few times, the pain inside causing his body to clench up before fully vomiting.

The detective was not worried about passing vehicles or witnesses. In this neighborhood, the sight of a man kneeling over a bloodied body meant you looked away and drove faster.

Slowly, Crowder's moaning subsided enough that Carlisle could speak and be heard. The fact that the policeman stayed near his body and never looked away terrified Crowder almost as much as Carlisle's skill with a flashlight.

"Listen to me," Carlisle said. "I'm going to go sit in my car until you can stand up and get in this piece of shit. You are going to drive away and never come back. Ever. You aren't going back to get your things from Diane Lansford's house. You hear me? You're done here. Forever."

"Aaagghh," Crowder said.

"If you're asking whether or not I'll kill you, the answer is no," Carlisle said. "I'm a cop. Though I will, and this is a promise, make sure your crew— and I mean Brady—finds out you're nothing but a snitch. We record you every time you talk to us. Making a little mixtape for Brady would be pretty easy."

Brady was Dakota Brady, the leader of Crowder's crew and a man with a hatred for snitches and absolutely no sense of irony given that he was also a snitch.

Carlisle stood from his crouch, placing his hand on Crowder's groin to increase his momentum as he got to his feet. Crowder screamed loud enough to start the dog barking in the trailer park.

Two blocks over a bus would soon drop Jimmy and Kelly off, and they would pass this spot as they walked home. Carlisle did not want the Lansford children to see Crowder lying on the ground. He took a pair of rubber gloves from his back pocket and pulled them over his hands. Crowder's blood was everywhere, and Lord only knew the nastiness in it. The Lord, and perhaps the free county healthcare clinic.

Carlisle squatted down, grabbed Crowder, and lifted him up in one rough motion, leaning him against the bed of his truck. Carlisle opened the driver's side door and grabbed Crowder again, this time manhandling him into the cab.

Carlisle said one word before closing the door.

"Drive."

Crowder slumped in his seat. Seeing the man's eyes roll back in his head, Carlisle worried that he might have gone too far. Then Crowder reached toward the ignition, started his truck, and pulled away. The old Chevy weaved back and forth between both lanes, mimicking the unsteady walk of a man whose gonads had just been crushed by a police department-issued steel flashlight.

Once his taillights faded from Carlisle's sight, Crowder was gone for good. No one in town saw or heard from him again, though Carlisle was sure he picked up right where he left off in some other town, minus the mooching-off-women part. It was hard to mooch off even the loneliest of women when he could no longer function the way his competition could.

Carlisle didn't violently intervene in Jimmy and Kelly's life again, but he did watch over them. He replaced Jimmy's Nikes later that spring. In Jimmy's junior and senior year, Carlisle and his new girlfriend Claudia had the Lansford children over for Thanksgiving. It was the first time Jimmy and Kelly participated in a real holiday. It was the first time they had anything to be thankful for on Thanksgiving—other than each other.

Jimmy never saw so much food in his life, and none of it came from a box or plastic package. When Claudia offered him and Kelly Tupperware containers full of mashed potatoes, turkey, and pumpkin pie, they politely declined, unable to stomach the thought of their mother taking the leftovers while cursing her children out for daring to have Thanksgiving without her.

But Carlisle's most important contribution to Jimmy's life wasn't the violent expulsion of Roger Crowder, new Nike running shoes, or homemade mashed potatoes on Thanksgiving. His most important contributions were the conversations about Jimmy's grades and his preparation for the ACT, and his presence at every cross-country meet he could attend. He would stand next to Kelly, a uniformed police officer and a beautiful teenage girl cheering a boy who often came in first. It was Carlisle, through both his words and his presence, who helped Jimmy start to picture a world beyond Garrity, a world where streetlights and mothers worked like they should.

When he looked at Jimmy, Carlisle was reminded of bare-knuckle boxing with his own father. Eldridge Carlisle fed his oldest son a bunch of backyard bullshit about the role these fights would play in molding him into a man. From the first swing Carlisle knew better. Their boxing matches were just a way for Carlisle's dad to introduce his son to an old man's bitterness and regret, formed in the shape of two calloused fists. Carlisle could have destroyed his father but didn't. He was far prouder of his ability to take a punch.

Though they never said I love you, not when they were young, both

Carlisle and Jimmy possessed the abused child's knowledge that words are cheap. Carlisle's father told him how much he loved him five minutes before he broke Carlisle's collarbone. Diane would tell Jimmy and Kelly how much she loved them right before she told them they wouldn't amount to shit.

Just like their father.

Love is expressed in all sorts of ways, words being the least important among them. He couldn't say the words, so instead Carlisle observed from a distance, sometimes seen, sometimes unseen, trying to do everything he could.

Trying to keep Jimmy and Kelly from falling into the darkness that existed right inside their own home.

CHAPTER ELEVEN

2019

The day began with Jimmy's usual routine: a cold Red Bull, one of Jill's homemade granola bars, and a seven-mile run around his neighborhood. Once his run was over, he would come home, shower, and—weekend or weekday—put on a pair of pleated khakis and a collared shirt.

By late afternoon that day, Jimmy's life would be disrupted by a crazed dash to Walmart for an Ouija board. However, the first disruption occurred when Jonathan met him at their front door in basketball shorts and a flat-brimmed Suns hat with the sticker still on the bill. He and Jonathan were essentially the same height, give or take an inch, so Jimmy didn't have to look up or down to see the fear in his son's eyes.

"Dad, did you put the mud in your room?"

Jimmy didn't know what his son was talking about. Jonathan stepped back to let his dad pass through the entryway.

"No? Mud—what do you..."

"There's mud all over your bedroom. Piles of it"

"Mud? I—Where's mom?"

"She took Jessica to volleyball practice."

Volleyball. The latest in their attempt to interest their daughter in sports. He could already tell volleyball was going to be just like gymnastics, which was just like T-ball: a way for him and Jill to waste time and money driving all over North Phoenix as Jessica scowled through practice, waiting for the drive home to tell her parents how team sports were another way for the patriarchy to reinforce its dominance over women.

"What mud are you talking about?"

"Come with me," Jonathan said, leading Jimmy up the stairs to the second floor and the master bedroom.

"Jessica clogged the downstairs toilet again. I was going to use your bathroom, and I saw this," Jonathan said as they entered the master bedroom, pointing to several piles of mud. The piles led from just outside the closet door to the bathroom in his and Jill's room.

"I didn't do that," Jimmy said. "Come on, Jonathan. You know I wouldn't just leave mud on the floor."

Left unspoken between father and son was that Jill would be angry at whoever left the mess. When Jimmy and Jill met in college, one of her most appealing qualities was her cleanliness.

"Well, if you didn't leave the mess, who did?" Jonathan asked.

Jimmy walked farther into the room, squatting down to get a closer look at the floor. They weren't piles. They were more like rough rings with hollow middles.

"Dad, Zach's waiting for me," Jonathan said. "We're going to play basketball."

Jimmy looked back at the drying mud on his floor, noting how it spontaneously appeared just outside of the closet, went into the bathroom, and then abruptly stopped.

"Dad? Hello?"

"Um, yeah. Go ahead. Tell Zach I said hi," Jimmy said.

Jonathan began to leave the room when Jimmy looked up and said, "Hey, buddy? You don't need to worry. No one is in our home. No home invaders, I mean. This isn't *The Strangers*."

"It's okay, dad," he said. This is what happens when you get old, he thought, looking at his dad sniff the floor. You just go straight crazy. "I'm grown up. That stuff doesn't scare me anymore."

Jimmy remained in his room as he heard his son's footsteps echo through their quiet home. The dirt was the only sign of disruption in his and Jill's bedroom. The bed was immaculately made, the drawers and bedside tables topped with framed pictures of their family: Jessica on Jimmy's shoulders on the beach the year they went to Disneyland. Jimmy in full makeup, his six-year-old son and three-year-old daughter giving him the makeover they knew—despite his protests—he wanted.

Jimmy looked at the mess again.

His perfectly photographed life disrupted by mud that seemed to appear from nowhere.

He placed his right foot, still clad in his bright white Nike running shoes, next to the pile closest to the closet door. He then stepped forward, his left foot landing near the pile second closest to the door. He took another step. Then another. And another.

These weren't piles at all.

They were footprints.

Jimmy looked at the bottom of his shoes. They were clean. He looked at the mirror above the dresser on Jill's side of the bed. There was no smudge, though looking at his own reflection caused a cold chill to run up the length of his back. He bent down again, getting an even closer look, his nose practically touching mud.

The air conditioner kicked back on.

Jimmy jumped to his feet, looking in the mirror. Still, nothing, though he was weeping. Again.

His eyes traced a line back to their bedroom door. He did not see a single speck of dried mud outside the piles. He started moving, tracing his steps back out of the room, going all the way downstairs to the front and back doors. Everything was clean, not a single speck anywhere else in the house.

Jimmy weighed his options. He could get the vacuum out and clean, telling Jonathan later he forgot and wore dirty shoes in the house.

"Crazy dad," he would say. "Must be getting older. Can't even remember what shoes I wore."

Or, he could show Jill how tenuous his grip on sanity really was by pointing out footprints that appeared to have no explanation.

He sat down on the couch in the living area and closed his eyes. He weighed the choice of carrying a secret alone or looking and sounding like a madman.

The air conditioner cooled his sweaty skin as he silently cried.

He wasn't sure how much time had passed when he felt the muscles and organs of his middle section trying to simultaneously retain and expel everything in his torso. His throat dried, and he felt pressure on the back of his eyeballs. Though he didn't notice it, he peed a little, a quarter-size drop of moisture visible on his grey shorts.

"Hello?" Jimmy asked. Tears leaked through his closed lids.

"Hello?"

Every light on the second floor sputtered until it flickered on, the glow in each slowly intensifying. Jessica's hamster—a fat, ugly, white-and-brown male his daughter named Lady Gaga—began throwing itself against its cage until the whole unit tipped on the floor and the door popped open. Lady Gaga ran for it, looking for the closest couch cushion he could find. A free-range hamster was the most chaos this house had ever seen, though things were about to get a lot worse.

"What do you want from me?"

The couch settled into the carpet as the light directly above Jimmy blew out.

"Please. Please," he moaned. "Tell me what you want."

He could feel slight pressure against his right shoulder.

"WHAT DO YOU WANT?"

Jimmy's eyes darted back and forth beneath his closed lids.

"WHAT DO YOU WANT?"

"WHAT DO YOU WANT?"

"WHAT DO YOU WANT?"

"WHAT DO YOU WANT?"

"WHAT DO YOU WANT?"

"WHAT DO YOU WANT?"

"WHAT DO YOU WANT?"

"WHAT DO YOU WANT?"

"WHAT DO YOU WANT?"

Jimmy closed his eyes tighter. Orange bursts of light fired behind his eyelids. He felt himself grow lighter. He kicked off his shoes and dug his toenails into the carpet, his feet searching for the grip his mind was losing. He knew, immediately, that he wasn't headed toward the outer reaches of cold space.

He was headed somewhere far worse.

Garrity, Oklahoma.

Soon he would float over the badlands of eastern New Mexico and north Texas toward the outskirts of his old hometown. There he and his companion would stand in the same spot his father stood when he took his own life. After that they would float to a different part of town, the part of town where a woman Jimmy shared DNA with once used the passenger seat of a decaying Firebird to earn the drugs she needed and the money she wasted.

His body remained rooted to the couch, but Jimmy's soul did not. It burst through his ceiling into the flat-blue Phoenix sky. Beige, brown, and blacktop as far as Jimmy could see rolled out beneath him. It was beautiful, all of it: the many, many Subways serving sandwiches in their master-planned neighborhood, new cars indistinct and parked only in driveways and garages, the Applebee's and the Barnes & Noble, all of it possibly signs of a culture in decline, all of it—even the Old Navy—a sun-scorched blanket of beautiful Jimmy chose, all of it new, all of it inherently incapable of holding a memory more than five years old.

"I'M NOT GOING BACK! I'M NOT GOING BACK! THERE'S NOTHING THERE! THERE'S NOTHING THERE! THERE'S NOTHING THERE! THERE'S NOTHING THERE! THERE'S NOTHING THERE! THERE'S NOTHING THERE!"

His forward motion stopped. Jimmy hung suspended, able to see how all the homes in his neighborhood have pools and perfect backyards mowed and manicured by hired landscapers. Expensive, clean, tidied, and cared for: It was the world he and Jill built and populated with people they both loved.

It was a world he would not leave. He would end it here, if he had to. He would reach back and clip his own wings if it meant not having to return to Oklahoma.

"PLEASE DON'T MAKE ME GO! PLEASE DON'T MAKE ME GO! PLEASE DON'T MAKE ME GO! PLEASE DON'T MAKE ME GO! PLEASE DON'T MAKE ME GO! PLEASE DON'T MAKE ME GO!"

Jimmy was no longer floating above his home. He was screaming the same words over and over, alone on his couch. He was soaking wet. From his scalp to his toes, streams of sweat rolled south. The skin of his palms was broken and red from his clinched fists.

In his terror, he failed to realize his companion was gone.

Perhaps it had done enough damage. Or perhaps it heard the downstairs door opening, Jill's Saturday morning sneakers echoing across the hardwood as she ran upstairs toward the sound of her husband's screams.

Jill reached the top of the stairs and saw Jimmy sitting on the couch with his eyes closed, his fists clenched. She saw the whites of her husband's knuckles, his bloodied palms, the way he appeared to have just climbed out of a swimming pool.

"Jimmy? JIMMY?!"

He opened his eyes and saw his wife standing there, her eyes wide, her upper lip trembling.

She dropped the Whole Foods bags and crossed the room, sitting next to her husband and taking him in her arms. He dug his head hard into her breast, needing a mother as much as he needed a wife. There was nothing there, she told him. No one was going to take him anywhere, least of all away from his wife, his children, and their home. She spoke the words she knew he sometimes needed to hear.

"You're safe," she said, pulling his head toward her shoulder.

"You're safe," she said once more, kissing him on the forehead.

She didn't know who Jimmy was screaming at. She was sure they were the only two in the room, and that prior to her arrival Jimmy had been alone. Just weeks ago, Jimmy was so controlled in his polite gentleness that sometimes Jill wished he could just relax and feel safe.

Now, looking at him, she wasn't sure how safe he was. She worried the human heart and mind could take just so much until it broke.

"You're safe, babe. You're safe, Jimmy," she said, again kissing him on the forehead.

Jill said the Lord's prayer from memory. Neither one of them would call themselves devout, but the words seemed to settle Jimmy down a bit, though it frightened Jill the way Jimmy squeezed her when she spoke the words, "Deliver us from evil."

If she were being honest, she would admit Jimmy scared the shit out of her lately, and that wasn't the sort of language she typically used. It was so bad that if Jimmy told her he believed a demon arrived from his childhood, and that demon was real, it would be somewhat of a relief.

Better a real-life demon than your husband rapidly losing his mind.

But years of marriage taught her honesty wasn't what she or Jimmy needed right now. She needed to believe that in the long run her husband would be okay, that this was some sort of temporary breakdown. She needed to believe that.

What did Jimmy need?

He needed to be around people who loved him.

He needed family.

CHAPTER TWELVE

2000

The letters began arriving in the spring of 2000. The University of Oklahoma, Oklahoma State, Rogers State, and the University of Tulsa all accepted Jimmy. Even a confirmation letter for enrolling in community college would make Jimmy the most academically successful Lansford in the history of Lansfords.

Letters from OU and OSU were on another level.

Most days Kelly got home before Jimmy, who usually had cross-country practice or student council after school. She would run to the mailbox, grabbing any letter with a college logo and hiding it from their mother until Jimmy came home.

Feeling the weight of his college acceptance packets made Kelly so happy for her brother. She was happy for herself, too. For the first time someone actually wanted them. After a lifetime of rejection that began the moment Diane realized she had missed a period, Jimmy and Kelly weren't just wanted—they were being recruited, and though her brother's name was the only name on the mailing label, she knew that when you got one Lansford kid, you got both. They were a "they," and they were leaving Diane's shadow for the light of a warmer world.

Kelly's excitement meant Jimmy couldn't tell her the truth about the letters. Though any school would be happy to have a cross-country state champion with a 28 on his ACT and a 3.8 GPA, cross-country was not football, a 28 was not a 36, and a 3.8 was not a 4.0. Every school offered a scholarship, but in each case the amount was short of what Jimmy needed to make his college dream a reality.

As the letters and disappointment piled up, Jimmy turned to the only person he knew—other than his teachers and coaches—with a college degree.

On an April day, Carlisle and Jimmy sat in front of Derry's. Carlisle looked closely at each letter and the financial aid packages offered. He could give Jimmy a motivational speech, tell the boy all he needed to do was believe in himself. He wouldn't do that, though. Carlisle treated Jimmy like a man—and a man knows wishing the numbers added up right doesn't make them add up right.

"I have an idea," Carlisle said.

"Yeah? Rob a bank?" Jimmy asked.

"An inside job? A cop? I like it. But it would never work."

Carlisle solemnly shook his head, as though he had briefly given bank robbery serious consideration.

"Why not?"

"Because I don't trust you as a getaway driver, Jimmy, and the Camry is too slow. That, and the bank people know me."

"Everyone knows you."

"Exactly. Bank robbery, out," he said, making a slashing gesture across his throat.

"Okay, then what was your idea?" Jimmy asked. Though his new and struggling goatee couldn't match Carlisle's, it was most visible in the bright daylight with a bit of ice cream in his chin fuzz.

"I played ball at OU with a guy who coaches at Arizona State. It's down in Phoenix. I could put in a call for you, see if my buddy can pull some strings."

Phoenix: a completely attainable city for most people, but the rich side of Paris for Jimmy. Even if he could somehow get out and make it somewhere like Phoenix, he would miss the man sitting across from him.

Carlisle seemed to sense what Jimmy was thinking.

"Look, my man, we'll be friends wherever you are. I'll come see you. But you need to get an education."

"How will Kelly—"

Carlisle waved a hand, his class ring from OU glinting in the flat Oklahoma daylight. He hadn't worn it in years but had slipped it on as he left his apartment, just for this conversation. It was gaudy, thick, dated—and earned. He assumed it was the first unpawnable jewelry Jimmy ever laid eyes on. He was right.

"It's no different at ASU than it would be here. If the scholarship requires you to live on campus, just ghost them."

"What?"

"Ghost them. Make yourself invisible. Take the scholarship and the dorm," Carlisle said, eating the last bite of his cone, "and get an apartment off campus. You and Kelly will have to work, but you guys have to work now."

"How will I get there?"

If Jimmy attended school in Oklahoma, Carlisle could drop him and Kelly off at their apartment door. Phoenix was different. He couldn't ask Carlisle to make a thousand-mile drive, and he didn't know how to get around Phoenix once he got there.

Carlisle fished around his pocket, pulling out the key to his 1987 Toyota Camry. Carlisle passed the key across the table and said, "When the time comes, take this."

"What? I can't take your car."

"Jimmy, you can take my car, and you will take my car. I spend most of my time in the cruiser, and the Camry is about done. It won't help you with the ladies, that's for sure," he said, laughing. "Claudia told me I needed to stop acting like I'm still a poor kid from Nowhere, Oklahoma, and get a grown-up car. But she'll still run. The Camry, I mean. She'll get you to Arizona. And once you're some rich investment banker, you can pay me back. It's not a gift. It's a deferred loan."

Jimmy sat face-to-face with a substance so rare it almost exists in the same universe as the precious metals of comic book science: unobligated love. He didn't know what to say, but he had the good sense to recognize the rarity before him, and just as he did that day in the barn, he opened his eyes wide and took the full view in.

"What do I need to do? I mean, to get into ASU?" he asked, hoping he masked the wobble in his voice.

"Apply, just like you did for the schools here. Once you've sent in your application, give me a call and let me know."

Jimmy did his part, submitting his ACT scores and transcripts to Arizona

State. In the essay he wrote about overcoming adversity, he did not mention his father's death, his mother's addiction, or the fact that he raised his little sister. He knew kids who made a mountain out of some relatively small tragedy in their application letters: the death of a distant cousin, a Godparent's leukemia diagnosis. Jimmy wouldn't do that.

He would not take someone's pity, would not be some college admission officer's charity case. Instead, he wrote an essay about training to become a champion cross-country runner, about willing yourself through the last mile of a long race. If a school wanted Jimmy Lansford enough to pay for him to be there, it was going to be because he was fast and smart—not because he was the child of screw-ups.

After Jimmy submitted his application, Carlisle did what he said he would do. Tim Deaderick coached the Arizona State baseball team. Carlisle and Deaderick had once been the poorest kids on the OU baseball team. In those days, Carlisle supplemented his scholarship with a job in the school's cafeteria, and every time Tim Deaderick came through the line Carlisle put extra meat on his friend's grilled ham and cheese. Deaderick supplemented his own scholarship with a job at a department store in downtown Norman, where he would set aside damaged t-shirts and jeans in Carlisle's size.

It was the first time anyone had Tim Deaderick or Mike Carlisle's back.

Tim Deaderick put in a word to ASU's cross-country coach, called in a few additional favors of his own, and five weeks after Jimmy submitted his application he received a packet from Arizona State University. It was, for the most part, the same as the packets he received from the Oklahoma schools, filled with glossy brochures and a letter that began with the words "We are happy to inform you."

There was one important difference, however, and that was the number that came after the words "expected family contribution." The number on that line from each Oklahoma school was small, and for most families more than manageable. For Jimmy, even a small contribution was a deal-breaker.

The number on the expected family contribution line in the Arizona State packet was zero.

As Jimmy stood in his room looking at the letter, a now fifteen-year-old Kelly by his side, his eyes welled up. They were going to leave Oklahoma on a maroon and gold magic carpet—Aladdin with a street-urchin sister in place of Jasmine.

In the living room, their mother screamed at Pat Sajak while ashing her cigarette on the carpet. This was a habit of hers, the floor around the couch pocked with burn marks. Though Diane's looks hadn't faded, the unexplained disappearance of Roger Crowder left her more bitter than ever. In her mind, Roger displaced Ronnie as the great lost love of her life. Diane blamed her children for driving away both of her men.

"We're leaving," Kelly whispered, leaning against her brother. Neither one of them had ever seen anything as beautiful as Arizona State maroon. "We're leaving."

"What do you think Phoenix will be like?" Jimmy asked.

Kelly looked down the hallway toward their mother, then out their bedroom window. Her brown eyes passed over their patchy yard, crossing the rutted street to the first plywood-windowed mobile home—and then soared skyward, past the Garrity city limit sign, over Interstate 40, across the rolling green hills in better parts of Oklahoma, past cowboy-hatted Amarillo, across the sagebrush of New Mexico, over the snow-capped mountains in Northern Arizona, and down Interstate 17 until the air became warmer and warmer, until her gaze pulled into a nondescript apartment complex with nondescript community mailboxes and nondescript people who simply left you alone—or, even better, occasionally said hello.

"Better," she said. "It will be better."

Diane took notice of the love and light down the hallway. It was hard to miss, the room pulsing with something wholly alien to her: unobligated love.

That night, after Jimmy looked around their room to consider what he would take with him to Arizona (almost nothing, he decided, just his clothes and his trophies) and had fallen asleep, Diane crept in and sat on the side of his bed.

"Wake up," she said.

He didn't wake up. There were few times in his life when Jimmy Lansford slept happy and exhausted, and this was one of them.

"Wake the fuck up, Jimmy," Diane hissed, punching him in the side.

"Huh, what?? What are you doing in here? Mom?"

Diane sat on the edge of the bed, her sleeveless yellow Def Leopard shirt practically glowing in the dark. She took the last drag of a cigarette and stubbed it out on Jimmy's dresser. She long ago stopped caring if she burned the house down. In her drug-addled brain, she assumed a fire might even bring insurance money. She was wrong. Diane's only claim on their home was a Section 8 voucher.

"Follow me outside," she said.

Jimmy waited until she left before getting out from under the blankets. He always wore sweatpants and a t-shirt to bed, aware that despite their closeness, he was sharing a room with his teenage sister. He could not sleep in his boxers like his friend Brian did. He looked over at Kelly, still sound asleep. He slipped on his Nikes and walked down the hall, knowing his mother would be on the back porch, smoking and looking out at their backyard and the Firebird.

Jimmy opened the door and stepped outside. Diane kept her back to him.

"Big man, huh?" She said, her back still to him.

"What?"

"Big man thinks he's hot shit. Just like his father. Ha!"

More than anything, Jimmy was bone-tired of this woman and her hunchback soul.

"Mom, what are you talking about?"

She turned to look at him, the Arizona State letter in her hand.

"You think you're going to college? Big man thinks he's going to college? You aren't better than me. You aren't smarter than me."

Jimmy lunged at the letter, and Diane jabbed his forearm with the lit end of her cigarette. He refused to grimace or show any pain. He knew it was wrong to be proud of being able to take a cigarette burn, but he learned at an early age that reacting in any way would only result in another burn. He also knew in his bones that any idiot can throw a punch—Ronnie did it all the time—but only a man can take one and get back up.

"Where did you get that?" He asked.

"You think I don't know you two hide shit from me?"

Looking at her made Jimmy feel the acid start to gather in his throat.

"I don't want to do this, mom. Can I go to bed?"

For once in his life Jimmy wished she would go to the Firebird, open a few beers, and put herself to sleep.

"Jimmy Lansford. Let me tell you something. I don't give a FUCK where you go to school. Go to fucking college in Alaska for all I care, you selfish fucking INGRATE. I put food on your table and a roof over your head and don't even get a fucking thank you. You just leave me. Fine. Fuck you. I don't love you, either."

"If you don't care, then why are you out here talking to me?"

"Because I don't give a fuck where you go, but you're not taking her with you," Diane said, motioning her jaw toward the house.

So that's what this is about, Jimmy thought. A custody fight. With his own mother. Over a kid she appeared to be indifferent to, except when she ordered Kelly to "make me some fucking eggs."

"Oh, I am. I am taking her," Jimmy said. "Kelly's coming with me."

"The fuck she is."

"Why do you even want her? You don't care about us. You never have."

"Oh," she said, trying on her flirty voice. The sound of it made Jimmy's stomach rise even farther in his throat. "Is my baby boy jealous that his sister is mommy's favorite? Do you want to be mommy's favorite? Do you?"

"Stay away from me," he said. Then, he added something he wanted to say for a long time. "Me and Kelly would be better off if you killed yourself like dad."

She flicked what was left of her cigarette at Jimmy, the lit end missing his ear, and laughed. Jimmy could not understand—would never understand—how a person came to be like his mother. Or his father.

"You don't think I wish that too? You don't think I want to put a knife in my own eye, like your piece-of-shit father did?"

"What do you want, mom? You want Kelly to stay? Here? In this house? With you? She's coming with me. End of story."

She lit a fresh cigarette and took a long drag.

"You know," she said. "I don't think that is the end of the story."

"Fuck off, Diane" Jimmy said.

They played games like this before. He was tired and knew she would forget about Arizona State and Kelly coming with him as soon as she passed out. He walked by her, ready to go back to bed. As he grabbed the doorknob, Diane spoke again.

"You know, it isn't natural that the two of you share a room," she said. "The way you two are always in there. Keeping secrets. It's not right."

Despite everything, Jimmy never thought about killing his mother, of sending her to whatever hell held his father.

Until that night.

"Shut your mouth. Diane."

"Ha! Big man. Hot shit. You know, I'm pretty sure I heard some weird stuff coming out of that room. Moaning and whatnot. Were you touching your sister? You know, maybe I should call the police."

"You're sick. Why don't you call the police? I'll give you his number."

"You mean that black cop you're always with? No, I don't think I'll call him. I'm pretty sure he's in on it too. Him helping my son molest his own sister. Fucking pig. Fucking black pig."

"No one will believe you. You're a whore. And a junkie."

Her smile stretched wider.

"And you know what happens in houses where the mother is a whore junkie? All sorts of bad shit."

Jimmy knew how to use a weight plate to protect himself, in theory. He knew how to throw a punch, in theory. He knew how to use violence to make his point, in theory. Until that night, though, he never laid a hand on anyone, ever.

He grabbed his mother by her scrawny throat and slammed her against their home. A piece of siding broke free and dangled, one end touching the patio.

Jimmy had eighty pounds of hard teenage muscle on her. The sound of Diane hitting the wall set off the neighborhood Cujo, which set off the usual chorus of various degenerates telling each other to shut the fuck up. The sound of other human beings caused Jimmy to loosen his grip, though he did not free his mother.

Unfortunately, his hand loosened enough to allow her to speak.

"You don't get it. You're not a man. You're a little fucking boy. It doesn't have to be true. You were in the paper, you fucking dummy. If I say you touched her, you're done. Some fucking college in Arizona doesn't want to give a scholarship to a child molester. And your faggot cop friend? The one that likes you so much? If I say he helped, he's done."

Jimmy stepped back and released his mother. He looked her up and down. This thing before him was part of who he was. It made him want an entire blood transfusion.

"Miserable fucking bitch," he said. He opened the back door as she stood on the patio. Once Jimmy was in his room, she packed a pipe and smoked a little crystal on the couch, guarding against any black helicopters that might think of taking her daughter away. She owned Kelly, just like those fucks down the block owned that constantly yapping dog.

That night Jimmy lay on his bed, thinking of how to respond to Diane's threat. He survived and even thrived by being pragmatic, thoughtful, and knowing when to fight—and when to run.

He could call her bluff, accept his scholarship to ASU, and just take Kelly with him at the end of the summer, when he left. He could also preempt Diane and tell Carlisle her plan.

He could stay and wait to go to college when Kelly was a little older and could come without his mother stopping her. But he knew if he stayed and went later, he wouldn't have a scholarship to count on.

He could also stay and apply for the police academy. Carlisle's recommendation was sure to get him accepted. Without a degree, he wouldn't be future chief material, like Carlisle, but he would do okay. He would have health insurance, a retirement plan, a steady paycheck, and a job that mattered.

Things his parents never had.

If he just took Kelly with, there was a good chance his mother would turn him in for kidnapping. She was that vindictive. He knew there were limits to what Carlisle could do, and his intervention wouldn't end with a judge giving an eighteen-year-old custody of a fifteen-year-old. If Jimmy knew how Carlisle dealt with Roger Crowder, he might have had more faith in Carlisle's ability to come up with a creative solution to problems involving lowlifes.

He could stay, attend the police academy, and follow in Carlisle's steps. He wouldn't move to Phoenix, but maybe he would go to the University of Phoenix one day—he'd seen the commercials—and work his way up through the police department.

That's what he would do.

There were worse footsteps to follow in than Mike Carlisle's.

CHAPTER THIRTEEN

2019

Maybe heatstroke could explain the way she found him in the downstairs half bathroom during Jessica's birthday party: crazy-eyed, sweat-soaked, and vomiting in the sink. But heatstroke could not explain the unexplained Skype call with a friend back in Oklahoma. Heatstroke could not explain the way he just disappeared so often lately, his body at the dinner table hunched over his meatloaf and mashed potatoes, his mind and heart far away.

And heatstroke certainly couldn't explain what she just walked in on.

"Jimmy, be real, okay? Don't bullshit me."

"Yeah, I just—"

"I know. You already said you had heatstroke," she said taking his chin in her hand and pointing his face up so he could look her in the eye. Though Jimmy was eight inches taller than Jill, he liked to lie with his head on his wife's chest, the strands of his hair brushing her chin.

"Can I show you something?" He asked.

"Sure, Jimmy."

"And you promise not to think I'm crazy?"

Jimmy did not realize making people promise not to think you're crazy is the fastest way to make people think you are crazy.

"Um...okay."

"Come with me," he said, taking his head off her chest and standing up.

The Whole Foods bags still sat on the floor; Kale, grass-fed bison, and artisan mushrooms taking root in deep carpet. Jimmy and Jill stepped into their bedroom, standing side by side just inside the doorframe. The house was quiet, the air conditioner having gone silent.

"Do you see them?"

Jill looked down at a few piles of dirt leading from their closet to the bathroom.

"The dirt?" She asked.

Though she didn't say it, her tone conveyed the second part of her question: So that's what this is all about?

"Yeah, but do you see?"

"See the mess Jonathan made?"

"It wasn't Jonathan. He's the one who showed them to me."

"Those are footprints. Someone tracked mud in here."

"I know they're footprints, but it's not mud. It's dry. Look," Jimmy said, gesturing toward the piles. Jill walked over to the dirt and squatted down.

"Look. Do you see what's weird about them? Look again."

Unfortunately, there was nothing strange or suspicious about someone tracking dirt in the house and leaving the mess for Jill to clean up. Her son, daughter, and husband were thoughtful people, but they weren't saints. They were prone to tracking dirt in, leaving cupboards open, and taking monstrously huge bowel movements that clogged the toilet and then swearing they had no idea where the poop came from.

"Jimmy, you're going to have to tell me. I see dirt. I see no one cleaned it up. I don't see the mystery."

"Look at the way they just appear out of nowhere. Do you see dirt leading to our room? Where did this come from?"

"Babe, it's Jonathan. Or Jessica."

"I told you Jonathan showed it to me. And Jessica is at volleyball practice. Where did it come from?"

Jimmy believed the footprints hadn't come from Jonathan or Jessica. While Jill didn't think the mud arrived by magic, she didn't believe her husband was purposefully lying—which presented one alternative: Jimmy had lost his mind.

"Jimmy, I don't know where it came from, but you need to do something for me."

"What?"

"Lie down. Just rest. When you're feeling better we'll vacuum this up, figure out where it came from, and talk to whoever made the mess."

What was Jimmy going to say? There's a demon in the house? My father was possessed and that's why he killed himself? The demon in our closet is going to take me back to Oklahoma? Jimmy could not bring himself to say any of those words. As a grown man, he said the word possession to Carlisle. But he could choose to cut Carlisle out of his life. He had done it before.

Jill, on the other hand, was his wife. Words spoken in a marriage cannot be unspoken, so he wasn't about to say, "I think I'm becoming possessed by the family demon."

"Okay," Jimmy said. "You're right. You're right. I'll lie down."

Jill pushed her husband toward their large bed. She reached down, grasping the bottom of his shirt as he put his arms up in the air. After his shirt was removed, she untied his shoes. As she undressed him, she could feel the tight wires in his body go a little slack. She kissed his forehead before pulling the sheet and blanket up to his chin.

"I love you, babe," she said. "Get some rest, and we'll figure this out."

She closed their door and stepped out. Jimmy heard her pick up the spilled groceries and descend the stairs.

Jimmy stared through the dim light of an air-conditioned bedroom in 2019. Jimmy stared at a barn door in 1997. Jimmy lay on a bed, his naked back sweating into twelve hundred threads. Jimmy stood sandwiched between a rusty Firebird and an old farm truck. Jimmy heard a twelve-year-old girl getting dropped off in the suburbs after volleyball practice. Jimmy heard a twelve-year-old girl saying "Kay" as he placed headphones over her ears and played a Cyndi Lauper song. Jimmy saw a mother's face as Jill kissed his forehead and tucked him into bed. Jimmy saw his mother's face as she told him Kelly wouldn't be allowed to leave their prison of a home.

Jimmy was in his Arizona home, crying and clutching a bedspread. Jimmy was inside a barn in Oklahoma, walking toward his father's corpse.

He sat bolt upright in their bed. He bent over and put on the same sweaty t-shirt he used for his morning run, the same one Jill just removed. He grabbed his wallet from the nightstand and placed a single credit card in his pocket. He then bent down and laced up his Nikes before walking over to the second-story window that faced their street.

Right outside the window was the roof covering their porch. Eight feet down from the porch roof was their front walkway.

Jimmy listened for a moment for the sounds of his wife's footsteps.

Nothing.

He pulled up the blinds as quietly as he could. The window raised easily, the sills in Estancia Estates always oiled, always smooth.

Jimmy Lansford was a 37-year-old man who believed a demon was stalking him. Even worse, he knew he was not the man he once was. Demons or not, he had become the monster he feared most: an unstable parent. If he couldn't fix it, if he couldn't control his own life, he at least needed to understand what was happening.

He climbed through their bedroom window, careful to land on the roof above the porch. Though he was visible to anyone who looked, the eight-foot-high walls around each house long ago conditioned his neighbors to ignore what occurred outside the boundaries of their quarter-acre kingdoms—especially if it involved a neighbor in need. In his neighborhood, people knew a crazy-eyed man standing on his own roof meant you looked away and drove faster. Of course, they knew it without being told. This specific scenario was definitely not addressed in the HOA's bylaws.

He knew he could not linger.

Jill and now Jessica were home, and Jonathan could arrive any minute. The nearest Walmart was almost five miles away, but he figured he could find what he needed there.

It was one hundred and four degrees, fall having cooled the weather from its summer highs that could soften blacktop and close the airport. He stood on the porch roof for a moment, the sun beating down on his disheveled head. He closed his eyes, inhaling car-heater hot air in his throat and nostrils. Jimmy stepped to the edge and did the one thing he found almost impossible to do.

He jumped.

Of course, he half-expected to never touch the sidewalk, to soar upward until the pressure and lack of oxygen popped his skull like one of Jessica's ba-woons.

Instead, he plummeted straight to the ground, scraping his knee hard against the concrete. He stood up, saw the blood sacrifice to his pressure-washed front walkway, and ran—first with a limp and then steadily faster as he reached the main road to Walmart.

To say Jimmy ran through hell would not be an exaggeration. He had already run seven miles before the temperature crossed one hundred degrees, experienced out-of-body travel, had a breakdown, and climbed out of his bedroom window before leaping to his sidewalk. That was before his feet pounded the ground for several more miles.

Every breath brought still hotter air into his lungs. He felt like he had swallowed the entire car heater, the angles sliding down his throat like blurry YouTube videos of snakes eating cows. The blacktop next to the sidewalk seemed to push even more hot air toward him, and every passing car showered him with a fine, painful spray of dirt and gravel. Sweat rolled down his face, mixing with the tears in his eyes.

Jimmy didn't stop running until he burst through the front doors, the elderly greeter too shocked for her scripted hello. He ignored her completely and grabbed a bottled water from the first cooler he saw. He would pay for it on his way out, he told himself. Once steadied and hydrated, he headed toward the section he needed, passing men's toiletries, the makeup aisle, and the seasonal summer section where they sell floaties shaped like turtles and high-powered squirt guns.

Then, in aisle twenty-one, two shelves up from Candyland and three feet over from Pictionary, he found what he was looking for:

Ouija, by Hasbro.

He turned around and headed for the checkout, bypassing the opportunity to pay for the Ouija board using the self-service scanner. It was not typically the sort of mistake one lives to regret, but specialized regret was something Jimmy specialized in.

The young mother ahead of him buying feminine hygiene products and ear infection medication for her baby was, perhaps, having an even worse day than Jimmy—though he took no notice. He was sweating profusely and smelled like death.

It was his turn to pay. The cashier took a glance at the sole item on the checkout belt and looked at Jimmy, who ignored the cashier's look. If Jimmy was worried about impressing anyone, he would not have jumped out of his window and run five miles to Walmart for a Ouija board.

"Did you see a price on these?" The cashier asked.

"No," Jimmy said.

"Because the barcode isn't working," the cashier said, scanning the item again. He looked at Jimmy in an accusatory way, as though Jimmy wanted any hassles or snags in his midday purchase of a Ouija board.

"I think they're nineteen or twenty dollars. Something like that."

"Something like that? You don't know?"

Jimmy could be profane, though almost never in public, and almost never with strangers. On this day though, he would not tolerate judgment from a young man who made his living passing board games and lunch meat over a bar code scanner. Jimmy leaned in, close enough only he and the cashier heard what he was about to say.

"I don't know what it costs, dipshit. Why don't you ask the fucking thing?"

Jimmy raised his lip, revealing a sharp canine whitened by dental lasers and an adulthood of rigid dietary choices.

The cashier did not recoil.

He did not even blink.

For young Andrew Ferguson, this was a day he long waited for. He had bills to pay and three quarters of a high school diploma. He wasn't stupid, though. He was a human being and deserved better than the way he was treated by assholes wearing hundred-dollar shoes.

Assholes, in other words, like the sweaty, smelly asshole hassling him about a Ouija board.

Andrew picked up the phone near his register, the one connected to the store's PA system. He looked Jimmy straight in the eye and did not hesitate.

"Price check, can I get a price check on lane seven? Price check on a Ouija board," he stopped for a moment. His face had the dead-eyed look of a gunslinger who has waited his whole life for this particular shootout. "Price check. Lane seven. Middle-aged man needs his Ouija board. Price check. Aisle Seven."

There are few things that can make the bustling hub of capitalism that is a suburban Phoenix Walmart on a Saturday grind to a halt like a price check on a Ouija board. Reactions across the store varied. One elderly woman kissed her cross necklace and headed straight for the exit, sure the end was nigh.

One young father answered his seven-year-old son's question of, "What's a weeja board?" by answering the question the boy had asked the day before, which was, "Where do babies come from?" He decided if one must choose, it's easier to talk about sex than the devil.

Shoppers clutched anything they could grab: a shawl, the cross dangling from their neck, a spouse's hand. It was like a bad smell passed through the store.

Jimmy looked around. Every single cashier and every single shopper, as far as he could tell, stopped to stare at the middle-aged man who desperately needed a Ouija board and a shower. A few people snickered, but most could tell Jimmy was not someone picking up the game for his kids to use at a sleepover. He looked like he needed it like Linda Blair needed it.

Andrew Ferguson picked the phone up, preparing to ask for yet another price check. With Andrew's lips six inches from the handset, Jimmy ran for it, his sneakers squeaking on the tile floor as he dodged families with carts stuffed to the brim. He headed for the exit, forgetting he was about to technically shoplift the bottle of water he never paid for. He ran through the automatic doors, not slowing down as he sailed through the parking lot before hitting the road that led to his home.

The security footage that featured Jimmy Lansford in a Walmart was not just stored on a hard drive and forgotten. Security personnel, cashiers, and even supervisors gathered to laugh at the video. Right up to the assistant manager, every employee agreed Mr. Oujia Board had that one coming.

But once Jimmy left the parking lot, his starring role in the day's footage ended.

No one saw the way he vomited along the side of the road, doubled over and snarling as cars drove by, spraying gravel on his shins. The cameras didn't see the way he seemed to slink up to his own home, trying to avoid being seen by whoever was inside. They couldn't see the way he opened the door manually, lifting it just enough for him to lie on his belly, the hot driveway burning the skin on his legs as he slunk into his own garage, like an animal trying to burrow its way into a space where it didn't belong.

Once inside his garage, no camera witnessed what happened next.

But Jimmy's observer did.

The observer waited, aware its most important work would occur when Jimmy returned. The observer watched as Jimmy scanned the workbench along the right side of the garage. The tools kept there were clean and organized, with various saws, hammers, and shears hanging from hooks mounted to the wall. Both Jill's and Jimmy's vehicles were in the garage, their waxy shine showing Jimmy's reflection as he moved toward the bench.

The shine of the vehicles also revealed a smudge trailing a foot or so behind him. The smudge could easily be mistaken for a sloppy wax job done at the car wash Jimmy and Jill frequented—until it moved. The smudge paused as Jimmy rummaged through the contents of his work bench. As his right hand came back out of a drawer, the observer saw what Jimmy held in his fist.

It was a large flathead screwdriver, the tip shiny and sharp.

The headlights and taillights in the two cars pulsed softly, the displays on the radios briefly coming to life. Jimmy didn't notice. The hair on his neck stood straight up. He didn't notice that, either.

The screwdriver was not as sharp as the tools one might find in an old farmhouse barn, but with momentum, it would do the job. Jimmy pointed the tip at his right eye. He opened the lids as far as they would go, taking in the scene before him: the workbench, the barely used saw hanging from the wall, bits and pieces of a life intentionally constructed to avoid Jimmy pointing something sharp and deadly at his eye.

The pressure inside all eight tires sharply increased. Both car radios came on and stayed on. If anyone else walked in the garage at that moment they wouldn't be able to hear themselves scream as the air filled with a sound-swallowing static. The static rendered the car radios as good as mute. The overhead bulb flickered and turned on, the light breaching the boundary of its glass casing, illuminating every black cavity in the structure, even the nooks and crannies of car guts, parts so concealed they should have resisted any light.

Jimmy extended his arm as far away from his face as it would get, and then did a slow-motion, practice stab toward his eye, making sure the trajectory was correct.

It was.

Jimmy extended his hand again, and again swung the screwdriver toward his face, stopping mere millimeters from his eye. Though the screwdriver did not make contact, he could feel the weight of the steel on his pupil. He extended his arm again. The third time would do it. He would swing fast and hard with no intention of living life blind in one eye.

Every needle on every dial on every instrument, from the old-fashioned speedometer in Jimmy's car to the air pump Jonathan used to inflate basketballs, suddenly shot all the way right. The static abruptly died and was replaced by the sound of both cars playing a song from Jimmy's childhood.

Jill realized she hadn't checked on Jimmy since tucking him in earlier in the afternoon. She opened the door, saw the empty bed, and briefly saw her worst nightmare float into her frontal cortex. She walked into their closet to see if Jimmy was there, hanging from the sturdy, expensive light fixture.

Jessica sat in her room watching the new *IT* movie on her iPad with Finn Wolfhard in it. He was in *Stranger Things*, and Jessica loved *Stranger Things*. She secretly wished she could have had a *Stranger Things* birthday party, like she was a little kid again. The band her dad hired was cool, but she preferred a Demogorgon piñata.

Jonathan was walking home, angry that Zach beat him at basketball. Jonathan knew why Zach won. It wasn't because Zach was a better player. It was because Jonathan didn't have his Kyrie Irving shoes with him. They were in the attic, covered in dried mud. He knew how much nice shoes meant to his dad. He didn't want to let Jimmy down by mistreating something his dad couldn't afford when he was the same age.

The shoes had gotten muddy when he and Zach built a homemade Slip N' Slide. He had been searching for one of his dad's vintage ASU t-shirts, when he looked down and realized how much mud he'd tracked in the house. He had cleaned almost all of it when he heard his dad get back from one of the multiple runs he took that day.

Jill in the closet.

Jessica in her bedroom.

Jonathan walking up the driveway, thinking about the lie he told.

Except for Jimmy, that's where all the Lansfords were when Cyndi Lauper and both car alarms sent them running toward the garage.

CHAPTER FOURTEEN

Summer 2001

Unlike other students, Jimmy hadn't returned home for Thanksgiving or Christmas. He couldn't afford to. Everything extra he earned from his part-time job making milkshakes at The Chuckbox was sent back to Kelly, via Carlisle. His mother no longer qualified for welfare benefits. Diane's two years had expired without her ever setting foot in a classroom or attending a single job interview. Though Jimmy's money wasn't much, he made sure to mail Kelly a little for food and school clothes.

They agreed the moment Jimmy arrived back in town he would head straight to the tables in front of Derry's. A table at Derry's was the same spot, about a year earlier, where Carlisle and Kelly had convinced Jimmy to leave for Arizona State, even if he couldn't bring his little sister. When Kelly and Carlisle staged their intervention, Kelly did most of the talking.

"You have to go, Jimmy," she said, Carlisle staying silent for this part of the conversation. "I'll be safe, and mom won't keep this up forever. I'll be there, just...just not yet."

"I kind of want to be a cop," Jimmy said, looking toward Carlisle. Though Carlisle agreed to help Jimmy get into the academy—if that's what he wanted—the thought of his young friend having to deal with men like Roger Crowder on a regular basis made him hope Kelly could convince him to go.

"It's a full ride, Jimmy," Kelly said. "Take it. I'll be there as soon as I can."

Kelly reached across the table and put her hand in Jimmy's, her fingers interlocking with his. Carlisle watched this display of affection. It was a mature gesture, and the sort of thing both Lansford children weren't shy about. It was, like Jimmy's discomfort with asking for favors, another reason why he loved them both.

"Jimmy, I need to tell you something," she said, holding his gaze. "'Member when I bit Ronnie in the neck when he was going to hit you?"

"Yeah."

"Well, if you don't go, that day will seem like a picnic. Trust me, I will kick your ass."

Carlisle burst out laughing, and slapped Jimmy on the shoulder.

"Buddy, I will help her. You want to be a cop here? Go get your degree and come back. They'll make you chief," Carlisle said, dabbing his eyes as his laugh trailed off. "Heck, they'll make you my boss."

Though they would go back and forth throughout the summer—even after Jimmy accepted his scholarship—that afternoon at Derry's largely settled the matter. Jimmy would be a Sun Devil. He would bide his time in the desert, returning in summer until Kelly could join him in Phoenix.

Now, almost a year later, he watched Kelly and Carlisle settle into their table from across the intersection. Kelly saw Jimmy behind the wheel of the Camry and jumped up, her arm waving like something had come loose in her shoulder. The light turned green, and Jimmy pulled into Derry's parking lot. Carlisle stood from the bench as Jimmy parked the Camry. Though he wanted to give Jimmy a hug, he would wait his turn until after Kelly had her chance.

Kelly was sixteen now and had left behind the black velvet choker and butterfly clips she was so fond of just a year ago. Her hair was longer and her face more mature. It wasn't like Arizona State lacked pretty girls, but even on the streets of Tempe, Jimmy knew Kelly would stand out.

Kelly ran toward her brother, nearly knocking him over. For a year, even with the volume all the way up on her Walkman, everywhere she went Kelly could hear the squeak of the Firebird's shocks. She heard it while she sat at school, sketching cactus and sunshine on page after page of her notebook. She heard it when her mother was at The Pearl, sloppily waving her lighter to Whitesnake and waiting for her next backyard customer.

The squeak was especially loud when her mother was actually doing her thing in the Firebird.

Kelly stayed in Jimmy's arms. When Carlisle realized the embrace wasn't going to end soon, he walked over and patted Jimmy on the shoulder.

"Looking good, my man," Carlisle said. "Looking tan."

"It's sunny all the time there."

"Hot?"

"Yeah, hot."

"Life's hot," Carlisle said, squeezing Jimmy's shoulder. "Let's get some ice cream."

Jimmy told them about his first year at Arizona State. Most of the stories had already been told in letters and phone calls, but no one minded. It was good to hear their voices blend together: Kelly and Jimmy laughing, siblings finishing each other's sentences, Carlisle telling a police story about the time his new rookie partner chased a half-naked man through his own garden after an ill-informed neighbor called in a false burglary. Jimmy told Carlisle and Kelly about his races, 101 classes with three hundred students, the fraternities that tried to get him to rush. He even made a joke.

"I'm not doing the frat thing. If I wanted to hang around mean drunks, I could stay at mom's house."

Kelly found this joke hilarious. Carlisle gave it a courtesy chuckle. He understood their fondness for gallows humor.

"So, have you taught her to drive?" Jimmy asked.

Carlisle delivered thin envelopes of five- and one-dollar bills Jimmy sent Kelly, and she had his house, cell, office, and pager numbers. If she was ever in trouble, she knew who to call. Still, he could not drive around alone in a car with her like he could with Jimmy. Not before Diane's threat, and not after.

"No," Carlisle said. "I thought that's why you came back."

Kelly looked toward her big brother, eyes wide and smiling.

"Jimmy, are you going to teach me to drive? For real?"

Jimmy smiled back and looked toward Carlisle.

"I think I will. What are you doing today?"

"Gotta work, my man. Here, though," Carlisle said, fishing a twenty from his wallet. "Take this."

"I—"

"Take it, Jimmy. It's not a handout. I told you, it's an investment. One day you're going to be rich and buy me a Lexus and a retirement home down there in Scottsdale. Trust me. I'll owe you way more than you'll owe me."

Other than telling Jimmy he never knew what happened to Roger

Crowder, it would be the least truthful thing Mike Carlisle ever said.

"Can we go to the movies?" Kelly asked.

"Sure," Jimmy replied. "Carlisle, you want to get some lunch tomorrow? I'll pay."

"As an officer of the law, it is unethical and against department rules for me to accept gifts. We'll go Dutch. But I will definitely have lunch with you."

Jimmy thanked Carlisle with the half-hug he learned at college from some of the guys he ran cross-country with. Carlisle left, and Jimmy and Kelly got into the Camry and drove through town, listening to music and doing everything to avoid Diane's house. They went to Sonic and ate burgers and tater tots. They went to a Jennifer Lopez movie called *Angel Eyes.* They crashed a quiet antique store. They played skeeball in the arcade next to the movie theater. Jimmy used some of his savings to buy his sister new shoes at the mall.

"Won't mom just take these?" she asked, looking at her pair of Skechers. Like Jimmy's first pair of Nikes, they were already her favorite shoes.

Jimmy just smiled and wrinkled his nose at her. It was their signal for a secret. It was a signal they used since they were little. It was the signal Kelly used when Jimmy asked where she got the package of Oreos she bought for him after his first report card with all A's.

"Gotcha," she said.

When those Skechers weren't on her feet, they would remain hidden under her bed.

It was a great day, but like all good days, it would end. Before it did, though, Jimmy knew he needed to keep his promise and teach Kelly how to drive.

"I have a surprise for you. A gift," Jimmy said.

"What is it? Tell me. Tell me now."

"Nope. Then it wouldn't be a surprise. One more stop, then I'll give it to you."

They stopped at 7-Eleven, where Jimmy bought Twizzlers and banana Slurpees. Once they were back in the Camry, they headed toward a small development under construction just outside of town. Jimmy saw the same sort of houses in Phoenix: row after row of what appeared to be the exact same home, built in a neighborhood with a goofy name.

In Garrity, the development was called Evergreen Canyon by Prairie

View Homes, though there was no canyon and hardly any green. When they entered the new neighborhood, Jimmy pulled the Camry over to the curb and shifted the transmission into park.

"Ready?" he asked, sipping his Slurpee through his licorice straw.

"Ready for what?"

"Ready to drive?"

Kelly clapped her hands and opened the passenger door, crossing paths with her brother near the trunk before she got into the driver's seat. The moon provided light for the development, which still consisted of framed skeletons waiting for innards and skin.

"What do I do now?" Kelly asked, adjusting her seat. In her heart she wasn't behind the wheel of a 1987 Camry. She was Aladdin's street-urchin sister learning to fly the same magic carpet that had taken her brother somewhere better.

"First, put your right foot on the brake," Jimmy said, gesturing toward her feet. "It's the one on the left. Then, grab the gear shift—it's right here—and use your thumb to push the button. Next, pull it into drive. It's the one with the D."

They both felt the transmission thunk its way through each successive gear.

"Okay. Let your foot off the brake. For now, we're just going to coast, so you can get the feel of the car before you press on the gas."

They coasted through the development, headlights cutting through the shadows of half-constructed homes. A few coyotes crouched behind piles of plywood and drywall, disturbed by the invasion of outsiders.

"You're good at this," Kelly said.

"Good at what?"

"Teaching me to drive."

"Eh, it's just the way Carlisle taught me. It's the only way I know."

Their path led them to the front of the largest, nicest, most complete home in the development. Diane's entire home would likely fit in the garage like a vicious spider nestled in the armpit of an attractive woman.

"Press your foot on the brake," he told Kelly. She did, way too hard, and both their heads shot forward. They laughed. "Not like that! Easy, next time. Now, turn the headlights off. It's on the left side of the steering wheel. Sometimes it sticks. After that, turn the car off."

"Kay," she said. Kelly did as her big brother told her, and they sat in the dark, facing a large, six-bedroom home with an empty pool in the backyard.

"Are there houses like this in Phoenix?" Kelly asked. The moonlight shone in her eyes as she scanned the half-erected homes and piles of lumber.

Jimmy laughed. He hadn't explored his new city much, but he knew there were houses like this everywhere in Phoenix.

"Yeah, there are houses like this there. Bigger, even. And nicer."

Kelly could not imagine a home larger or nicer than the one she was looking at.

"Kelly," Jimmy said. "How are you doing? Are you really okay here, alone, with mom?"

Kelly looked at her brother.

She was not okay. Every night she cried herself to sleep. What was tolerable with Jimmy around was nearly unbearable with him gone. She had friends, and like Jimmy, was a popular enough kid. Like Jimmy, though, she could never bring friends home with her. In a town the size of Garrity, Oklahoma, the Lansford family's poverty and tragic history were well known. Her friends even saw her mother on the sidewalk downtown, waiting for some man to pull up and offer drugs or money.

But common knowledge was different than having a friend see a cloudy pipe and empty beer cans on a kitchen counter—or hear Diane call her own daughter a lazy bitch.

"I'm okay. Plus, we only have one more year. Next year I'll be seventeen, and I don't think mom will stop me from leaving. Just one more year, Jimmy."

Jimmy smiled, though her answer made him sad. He didn't need Kelly to wrinkle her nose to know she just kept a secret from him, the secret of how miserable her life in Diane's house was without her big brother around.

"Can I get my surprise now?" She asked.

"Yes. But first, I have to ask you a question. And it's going to be weird, but I know you like scary movies. So take me seriously. Please."

Kelly was a kidder, a joker, a shoulder puncher, and almost always sarcastic. She set her nature aside and did Jimmy the courtesy of taking him seriously.

"Okay, I will. Ask away," she said, taking a sip of Slurpee through her Twizzler straw.

"Do you think Mom and Dad could be possessed—or, I guess, do you think mom is possessed and dad was possessed? Like, maybe whatever it was moved from him to her?"

"Possessed, you mean, by the devil?"

"I guess so. Yeah."

Kelly wondered if a car like Jimmy's Camry would even be allowed in a neighborhood like this, once it was finished.

"Jimmy," she said, turning to look at him. She did not smirk, smile, or mock. "What would the devil want with mom and dad?"

"It's just—"

"No, seriously. I'm not teasing you. I believe in this stuff. You know I do. But if you were the devil, and you could leap into anyone's body in the world, why would you choose mom and dad? Is the devil just curious about what Milwaukee's Best tastes like? Does he need to learn how to steal cable TV? It doesn't make sense. I mean, seriously. Unless the devil has a craving for Spam, why possess Dad? And Mom? If the devil's inside of her, I feel bad for him. No one deserves that. Not even the devil."

Jimmy laughed.

"What?" Kelly asked.

"You...you just said 'inside of her.'"

"Real mature, Jimmy. And...actually, I was talking about your mom, so I kind of said inside your mom. Joke's on you."

Banana Slurpee shot from Jimmy's nostrils as they both laughed until their faces ached, until there was nothing more to laugh at.

Kelly kept looking out the front of the Camry. Jimmy watched her and knew one day both their worlds would expand. There would be friends, roommates, girlfriends and boyfriends, husbands and wives, children and grandchildren—but this girl, his sister, would be the only one who was once in the hole with him, not a shovel between them, fighting and figuring their way out. One day Jimmy and Kelly would tell others about the hole, and the people who loved them would feel for them, sympathize with them, even cry for them—and still have no idea what a hole that deep smells like, how hard you had to fight to breathe the dirt before it breathed you.

"Our parents are just shitty people, Jimmy," Kelly said, smiling at her big brother.

There was little more to say. Kelly presented a sound, logical argument.

And she made him spray Slurpee from his nose. His couldn't wait for her to get to Phoenix.

"If I was the devil," she said, "I would look for someone in a home like this. With a pool. And a big garage."

Jimmy couldn't argue. If Satan had any sense at all, he would come to a development like this, and stay far away from Diane Lansford's neighborhood, where competition for the worst person in town was too stiff for even the devil.

"Hey, let me give you your present," he said, reaching into one of the garbage bags he used for luggage. He pulled out a Discman. Attached to the Discman was a cord with a tape on the end. He plugged the tape into the Camry's radio. "This is a Discman. It's like a Walkman, but it plays CDs. And the tape lets you play it in a car radio."

"That is so cool! Jimmy, thank you so much. I love it."

"That's not all. I got you a CD, too."

"Who is it?"

"Willie Nelson."

"What? Jimmy, you know I hate country."

"Just try it."

Jimmy pushed the button that opened the Discman and placed the CD inside, closing it with a soft click. Through the Camry's speakers, Willie Nelson began to sing his version of "Time after Time."

They sat there, the Camry turned off, the interior lit by the moon. Even the finished houses around them were dark, the future occupants not yet having taken possession. They listened to Willie Nelson sing Kelly's favorite song five times in a row, Jimmy keeping the Discman still so Kelly's singing wouldn't be interrupted by the CD skipping.

They knew they couldn't avoid the inevitable. Eventually they had to return to Diane's house. Before they left, Kelly looked through the windshield and said, "When I grow up, I want to live in a house just like this."

CHAPTER FIFTEEN

2019

Cyndi Lauper and the car alarms were deafening, but they could not drown out a voice Jessica heard that said one word: "Go."

She dropped her iPad without even bothering to pause her movie and ran down the stairs two at a time, her mother right behind her. In the driveway, Jonathan punched in the code to open the garage door. Just as the door started to rise, Jessica and Jill entered the garage through the house. Jill found the car keys hanging on a hook and pushed the red PANIC buttons on each key fob, quieting the alarms. The music stopped, too.

Jonathan saw his father first. Jimmy was slumped on the ground, his back against the tire of Jill's SUV. His hair and t-shirt were soaking wet. He was shivering uncontrollably, despite the heat. Near his right hand, on the concrete floor, lay a long screwdriver.

"Jimmy. Jimmy. JIMMY!" Jill shook her husband by the shoulders. His eyelids fluttered, but he did not wake.

The temperature inside the garage when Jimmy did his practice run with the screwdriver was north of one hundred and thirty degrees. Jill stood and pulled her phone out of her pocket, just as Jessica stepped toward her dad. She dropped to her knees and inched close enough to smell Jimmy's horrible smell, close enough to feel his breath becoming irregular.

Jill watched her daughter, the hand holding her phone falling to her side.

Jessica placed her hands over her dad's ears, covering them for a moment before grabbing his shoulders. Jonathan grasped his mother's hand. The goosebumps on their wrists touched.

Jessica placed her chin just above Jimmy's collarbone, opened her mouth, and bit down on her dad's neck.

Her canines penetrated hard and deep enough to draw blood.

Jimmy's eyes flew open as he took a large, gasping breath. Jessica leapt backward. The last thing she remembered was watching her movie. Though she wasn't aware of it, her dad's blood was on her lower lip and shirt collar.

"Get him in the car! NOW!" Jill screamed. She, wisely, concluded Jimmy's family could get him to the ER faster than an ambulance could. Jonathan and Jill worked together, lifting Jimmy into the backseat. Jessica stood in a daze, not sure of where she was or how she got there.

"Jessica, GET IN THE CAR," her mother shouted. Jessica climbed in next to her father, pulling his sweaty arm over her shoulders.

Jill backed out of their driveway. She saw the exterior screen lying on the porch roof. He had jumped—and Jimmy was no jumper.

The last sliver of darkness visible between the garage door and the concrete floor disappeared as Jill put the car in drive. She drove as fast as she could, glancing back in the mirror every few minutes at her husband and daughter in the backseat. Jessica was still slumped against Jimmy.

Jonathan called the hospital as they drove. Upon their arrival, the ER team removed Jimmy from the backseat and placed his body on a stretcher. He was wheeled in, bypassing the normal intake procedure, and given an IV immediately. His pulse was dangerously low, and his breathing was still irregular.

The emergency room nurse also noted the bite marks on his neck. Jill didn't have an explanation and wasn't about to tell the nurse what she saw Jessica do. She just shrugged her shoulders. How could one account for bite marks on the neck of a man who was clearly in the midst of a breakdown?

Given how close he was to death, the nurse did not press the matter. There were more important issues at hand.

Jimmy was diagnosed with severe dehydration and heatstroke. He was given immediate fluids, and his body was immersed in a specialized cooling tub before being transported to his room. One emergency room doctor told Jill if they had arrived a few minutes later, her husband might not have survived.

"You know, it's a miracle your car alarms went nuts," the ER doctor said.

"Is he going to be okay?" Jill asked. She didn't know life as a real adult without Jimmy and didn't want to start knowing that life now. Or ever.

"He'll be here for a bit, but I think he's going to be okay. He should wake up soon," the doctor said. He went to exit the room, turning back once more to speak to Jill. "You know, your husband is a lucky man."

Jill offered Jonathan and Jessica the chance to go home. She could call Zach's mom, she said, and both could stay over at Zach's house before coming back to the hospital the next morning.

Neither of Jimmy Lansford's children was going anywhere. They made that clear to Jill. They all slept together in the small hospital room: Jill in a chair, Jonathan stretched out on the floor, Jessica curled up next to her dad, careful to avoid bumping the arm with IV tubes in it.

Though Jimmy was not technically in a coma, he still wasn't awake. The doctors assured Jill her husband could wake at any moment, so they all waited, getting little sleep—but getting little sleep together.

Around seven that morning, three knocks on their room door woke Jill from a nightmare.

She stood in an alley, looking into a backyard overgrown with weeds and tall grass. In the yard was a vehicle, though from her angle, she couldn't tell what the vehicle was, but it had the outline of an old sports car. There were no lights on in the street, and the alley she stood in was pitch black. Everything around her was lit only by the moon and weak light coming from a window in the back of the house she faced. The only sounds were a squeak as the vehicle moved side to side, and the relentless bark of a dog somewhere in the distance.

She was shaken up even after she woke and was glad to have Dr. Peter Gallagher, their family physician, bring her back to the real world.

"Jill, can I see you for a bit?" Dr. Gallagher asked, placing his hand on her shoulder as he entered the room. The doctor could tell she was jumpy, and who could blame her?

"Sure, sure," Jill said. She slipped her shoes on, looking at her children and her husband. Everyone who mattered most to her slept just feet away from a machine that showed the exact moment a human being leaves this world. She was glad to get a break.

Dr. Gallagher waited for her outside.

"Can we go get coffee?" he asked

"I could use it," she said, and followed him down the sterile blue-and-white hallway until they reached a waiting room with coffee and stale donuts. He poured her a cup, and the two sat opposite each other in the hospital's cheap, uncomfortable chairs. There were Kleenex boxes everywhere, and a blond-haired, blue-eyed Jesus observed their conversation from his spot on the wall.

Dr. Gallagher took a deep breath.

"Jill, what do you know about Jimmy's childhood?"

She couldn't see what Jimmy's childhood had to do with heatstroke.

"A little bit, but he doesn't talk about it. Hardly ever. I know his father committed suicide, and his mother died from liver failure. That happened while we were married. And—"

"I'm going to get right to the point—I apologize for being so abrupt, it's just—"

"No, go ahead. Please," Jill said.

"How familiar are you with survivor's guilt?"

"I've heard of it."

"Once upon a time, survivor's guilt was its own diagnosis. Now it's lumped under PTSD, but it's a specific kind of PTSD. A few years ago, Jimmy came in complaining of stomach pain. Remember?"

Jill remembered. Three years ago she would occasionally find Jimmy doubled over their toilet, clutching his stomach. It was so frequent—with no visible output, so to speak—that she asked him to visit Gallagher.

"Yes, I do."

"Did he tell you what the diagnosis was?"

"Some sort of ulcer, I think. He was pushing himself too hard at work."

Gallagher knew Jimmy and Jill well. Jimmy Lansford wasn't the type to just jump out of a second-story window and see if he could run himself to death in what, to Dr. Gallagher's knowledge, would be the second-oddest way to commit suicide he had ever heard of, the first being the way Jimmy's father took his own life. Gallagher never heard of anyone committing suicide like that.

"We couldn't find anything wrong with Jimmy. Physically."

Jimmy had told Jill he had a mild ulcer. Nothing to worry about, really. Just a gentle reminder that health is not solely defined by miles run; that's all the doctor had to say. According to Jimmy.

"What? No ulcer?" Jill asked.

"Nope. No ulcer. No tumor. Nothing, as far as we can tell. I referred him to a psychiatrist, Dr. Daniel Gera. I shouldn't be sharing this with you, because Jimmy didn't sign an authorization form, but as his family physician I have access to his records. When the hospital informed me Jimmy had been admitted, I thought it would be good for us to talk."

She hadn't expected to have a conversation about her husband's childhood as he lay recovering from heatstroke.

"Jill, your husband has perhaps the worst case of survivor's guilt I've ever seen. At least, with any patient I've ever treated. He was diagnosed with PTSD, but he refused treatment. He was quite honest with the psychiatrist, and said he was scared to take any sort of medication. Too many addiction issues in his family."

Jill reached for the tissue box.

"You said," Gallagher leafed through several sheets attached to the clipboard in his hands, "Jimmy has been acting strange for the last few weeks."

"Yes, but..." But what? She'd worried over him ever since getting the strange text about being safe in Cedar Rapids.

"Episodes of PTSD can be triggered by specific events. Is there anything that could trigger Jimmy? Sneaking out of your window and running for hours on a hundred-plus day is not...it's not healthy behavior."

"I...I don't know. The only thing I can think of is that when he and his sister were twelve and fifteen...I mean, that's how old they were when his father committed suicide. Jessica turned twelve just the other week."

"What does Jimmy say about his childhood?"

"Nothing. Or, not much. I know it was hard. I know they were poor. I know some old fireman looked after him and Kelly," she said, dabbing at her eyes. "Like I said, he almost never talks about it."

Jill finished her coffee, looked at the empty cup in her hands, then back up at Gallagher. "I know there's bad stuff back there. In Oklahoma. And I wish he would talk about it with me, but he won't. I just didn't know if I should push it. Or, you know, if that would make it worse."

"You should try and get him to talk about it with somebody," Gallagher said. "Because let me tell you something, as a medical professional. The human body can survive incredible trauma. You hear stories about people whose parachute doesn't open, and sometimes they walk away. The mind...isn't the same. It won't survive without a parachute."

Gallagher finished his coffee and stood to leave. Jill stood with him, shaking his hand.

"I'll check back on Jimmy and the rest of you later," Gallagher said. "Be well. Please get him some help. Your husband is a good man. A good dad. Tell him, when he wakes up, his kids deserve to have him around a while longer."

They shook hands, and Jill walked down the hall, her shoes echoing through the corridor. She kept her gaze focused straight ahead, knowing nothing good came from an accidental glance into someone else's hospital room. A few feet away from Jimmy's door, she heard Jessica.

"Dad, you should have seen it. You were almost DEAD. And the car alarms kept going off and Mom and Johnny—"

Jill's heart lifted. Though she couldn't hear Jimmy, she could hear Jessica filling him in on how they found him on the garage floor. Jill wondered if her daughter would remember biting Jimmy's neck. She hoped not. Something Jill didn't understand happened in her garage, and she was willing to leave it a mystery.

"Jonathan. Your brother's name is Jonathan," Jill said, correcting Jessica from the doorway.

Jill didn't care if her daughter called her brother Johnny or Jonathan, but she knew using Jonathan's full name was important to her husband. She stood just inside the room, looking at the man she built her life with. He looked tired and small, though his eyes looked less vacant than they had in weeks. Jimmy looked up at his wife and smiled, though moving his lips still took effort.

I love you, he mouthed.

I love you too, she mouthed back, moving toward his bed and the pile of people on it.

Jimmy would remain hospitalized for another twenty-four hours, his family never leaving his side. He began consuming solid foods later that day. Throughout his entire stay, he never experienced a single instance of floating outside of his body, never saw a smudge in any mirror. He never snarled at any of the nurses or doctors who treated him. He watched TV and rested and played checkers with Jonathan.

Jimmy was no less horrified by hospitals than the average person, but his time at McCain General was some of the best he'd had in a long time.

After checking out, a car full of Lansfords pulled out of the parking lot and made its way toward I-17. As they passed Happy Valley Storage, Jessica spoke up.

"Hey dad?" she asked.

It was her way of asking permission to ask a question. He was sure she would ask if he was crazy. If she did, he would answer his daughter honestly. He would tell Jessica he didn't know. Maybe. Maybe he was crazy.

"Can you tell me about Aunt Kelly?"

Jimmy looked in the rearview mirror.

Jessica smiled at her father and wrinkled her nose.

Jimmy spun around, looking his daughter in the eyes.

"Why do you want to know?" he asked, far too aggressively.

Jill placed her hand on her husband's forearm. Though all of Jimmy's childhood was a sensitive subject, his sister was the topic everyone knew to approach with the most caution. It was like sticking your finger in someone's open wound. That is, if your fingernail was especially sharp and the wound especially raw.

"Because I just...I don't know," Jessica said, looking out her window. "These last few weeks I've thought about her. A lot."

Jimmy looked at the houses they passed. When he was a kid in Oklahoma, a neighborhood like this might as well be Mars, and not because North Phoenix looks like Mars—if Mars were colonized by Red Robin franchisees.

Jimmy knew, after nearly dying right in front of his family, that he could no longer keep his past to himself. He took a deep breath and began to tell a story. It was the story of a boy and a girl, siblings born three years apart, just like Jonathan and Jessica.

These siblings grew up in a world and a home very different from the one Jonathan and Jessica knew. Their names were Jimmy and Kelly, and they lived in all sorts of places: Apartments. Cars. Tents. More apartments. A farmhouse on a dairy with an old barn. A rundown house in a rundown town in Oklahoma.

In each of these places Jimmy and Kelly protected each other.

Sometimes, when they were little, Jimmy would sneak into the kitchen of wherever they lived and find food for Kelly. When their father was angry—hitting angry—Jimmy would hide his sister under a sink or bed until the anger passed. When they grew up, or at least became teenagers, Jimmy still made sure his sister felt safe and protected.

But the story wasn't just about a big brother saving his little sister. Far from it. The little sister saved her big brother, too. Once—and this was a story only he, Aunt Kelly, and an old cop friend named Carlisle knew—the little sister jumped on their father and bit a chunk out of his neck, which saved the brother from a closed-fisted beating.

Jimmy did not see the look that passed between Jill and Jonathan as he told the story of the neck-bite.

Their father and mother were so mean the boy thought they must be possessed by the devil, but one time the sister explained how the devil would never possess their parents. The devil wouldn't want to eat Spam and steal cable TV. That made Jimmy laugh back when he heard it, and it made Jill, Johnathan, and Jessica laugh, too—even though this was a sad story, and they knew it shouldn't be funny.

Jimmy liked watching his family laugh at his sad stories. Sometimes you protected people with your teeth, and sometimes you protected people by making them laugh. Dark jokes are the best way to fight monsters. Kelly taught him that.

Their time together wasn't all sad, though.

Their Aunt Kelly loved music, Jimmy told them. She loved cool '80s bands. She really, really loved Cyndi Lauper. Her favorite was a song called "Time after Time."

At this point in the story, Jessica interjected, saying, "I know that song! I LOVE that song!"

"Well," Jimmy said, "your Aunt Kelly loved it too. Sometimes, when Diane and Ronnie—sorry, my parents—were screaming at each other, she would sing it so I could fall asleep."

Aunt Kelly was cool, Jimmy told them. And a little wild. Once, his friend Brian bought packages of Roman Candles, and Kelly had the idea to have a duel with the fireworks. (At this point in the story, it was Jill's turn to interject and tell Jessica and Jonathan to never, ever have a Roman Candle duel.) During the duel, Kelly shot Brian in the side of the stomach, and though the flaming ball burned through Brian's shirt and left a slight scorch mark on his ribcage, all Brian could say the next day to Jimmy was, "Man, your sister is awesome."

And she was awesome.

"Sometime," he said, "I will tell you a story about my friend Carlisle. He was the cop. He was Aunt Kelly's friend, too."

He told them about the way he and Kelly used to watch *Friends,* and how—like little kids—they pretended to be Ross and Monica, living together in a big city. He told them about race days, how Kelly would wake up early and make him eggs so he could get some protein before he ran; how she always clogged the toilet with her huge poops and how funny she thought that was, just like Jessica.

What he couldn't tell his family, no matter how many words he used and how many stories he told, was how Kelly was his person before they were his people. When you grew up like he and Kelly did, it didn't matter how many races you won or how many times you were elected to student council. Jimmy and Kelly couldn't let people into their home. When Diane Lansford's front door closed, the nightmare they lived became its own world. No one— no friends, no girlfriends, no boyfriends—could be let inside that world.

Jimmy couldn't tell his family, not in a way they would understand, how any light in Diane's home was created by the love between him and Kelly, like the spark of two sticks struck against each other at the very bottom of the deepest cave—and how dark that cave became when half the flame left Oklahoma for Arizona.

"But Dad, that was what you guys *did* together. What was she like back then?" Jessica asked.

"What do you mean, what was she like?"

"I mean, if you had to describe her. What was her personality like?"

Jimmy felt his throat catch. His eyes grew prickly and warm.

"She was like you, Jessica. Tough. Funny. A little crazy."

His daughter rolled her eyes.

"Not good enough, Dad. I mean it. What was she like?"

Jimmy steadied his voice. Outside his window the beige of their neighborhood came into view. He thought of the night he taught his sister to drive, and the way homes like his own still made him think of skeletons.

"You know pizza? Like, good pizza? The kind we get from Mellow

Mushroom?"

Everyone in the car nodded their head.

"And you know how pizza tastes at school? Like, even if it's bad pizza, it always tastes good at a school pizza party? Because it's out of context?"

Again, they all nodded. Jessica knew what context meant and was proud of herself for knowing such a big word.

"Well my sister was the best Mellow Mushroom pizza you've ever tasted. Extra cheese. All the meats. No mushrooms. Nothing gross."

Jessica smiled. She hated mushrooms.

"Your Aunt Kelly was the best possible pizza in the worst possible classroom. That's what she was like."

Though he had given Jill and the kids more details than he ever had about his sister, he would end this story the same way he ended every story about Aunt Kelly: by telling his family how sorry and sad he was that they never got to meet her, how much he missed her, and how much she would have loved all three of them—especially her niece and nephew. How they would have been her family too. He faced Jessica and told her how much she reminded him of her aunt.

And how happy that made him.

"Don't say 'would have been,' Dad," Jessica said, air quoting the three words she found offensive.

"What do you mean?" he asked.

"I mean, I don't like it when you say 'would have been.' Aunt Kelly is still part of our family."

It touched Jimmy that his daughter was so protective of a memory she never had.

Jimmy, Jill, and even Jonathan wiped tears from their eyes as the family pulled into their driveway. The garage door opened, and Jill thought there was something she was supposed to remember before she pulled in, something that landed on the garage floor as Jimmy fell. A hammer? The saw? Nails? What was it? She couldn't remember, and in any event, it was gone.

The garage floor was clean.

Each Lansford sat in the car an extra moment before they got out.

Jimmy hoped life would return to normal. Jill closed her eyes and said a silent thank-you. Jonathan promised himself he would spend more time with his dad.

Jessica stayed in the backseat and kept looking at the dark corner of the garage as her brother and mom helped her dad into the house. On one of the small shelves in the corner sat a flashlight, no more than four inches long. It wasn't the sort of flashlight you could use to crush someone's skull— or genitals.

It was a small thing, made specifically for the delicacies of suburban darkness.

Jessica watched as the bulb behind the lens began to glow bright and hot until the lens broke with a soft shatter. Slowly the interior of Jill's car became brighter as the tiny beam of a four-inch flashlight traveled through the windshield and transformed into an enormously warm, thrumming spotlight; a glowing, vibrating embrace of a young girl who still had a little of her dad's blood on her collar—a girl brave enough to step forward exactly when it was needed.

A girl who helped the light rescue someone they both loved.

Kelly Lansford's niece smiled, looked into the light, and wrinkled her nose.

CHAPTER SIXTEEN

Fall 2001

Carlisle reached for the buzzing Motorola on his nightstand.

"Mike," Sergeant Randy McCormick told him, "It's one of those Lansford kids. You might want to get out there."

McCormick was a friend in the department and knew about Carlisle's friendship with Jimmy and Kelly Lansford. Though Carlisle was cautious about who knew of his relationship with two teenage kids, it was an open and inconsequential secret within the Garrity, Oklahoma, police department. Carlisle's decision to look after the two children garnered the detective respect, not suspicion. No one in the department questioned Carlisle's integrity, though perhaps that had something to do with his abundance of caution.

Carlisle hurriedly put on his clothes, stubbing his toe as he searched for socks in the dark. Claudia woke from her sleep as Carlisle was pulling up his pants, her voice still groggy.

"Babe," she said, "is everything okay?"

"Gotta go."

Carlisle laced up his shoes and pulled his GPD windbreaker on.

"Mike. Hey. Is everything—"

"Gotta go, Claudia. I'll call you."

By the time he finished his sentence, he was shouting the last few words back into their apartment.

If anyone else in Garrity thought of a crime that defined the fall of 2001, it would be airplane hijackings almost fifteen hundred miles away. When

Carlisle thought of the fall of 2001, he wouldn't think of skyscrapers. He would think of a Pontiac Firebird found wrapped around a tree in the front yard of an abandoned home north of Diane's place.

By the time Carlisle arrived, there were already multiple officers on the scene, along with paramedics and firefighters. The driver, assumed to be Diane Lansford, had fled on foot.

Residents of still-occupied houses and trailers gathered on their porches and sidewalks to watch. With a car accident, there was no need to put your head down and walk faster. For once the neighborhood was brightly lit, the reds and the blues of various sirens making it practically like daylight, and the residents of this part of town were like the residents of any part of town: They weren't about to turn down a free show.

Carlisle stepped out of his cruiser and looked toward the mangled, faded black steel.

"Mike?" a young officer named Kyle asked. Carlisle turned his head, spotting a boy not much older than Jimmy in a police uniform. "Mike Carlisle? Someone told me you know the victim? I—"

Carlisle raised a hand to silence the young officer and walked around the rear of the Pontiac. Though there were people all around, the sound that registered to Carlisle was the incessant barking of a dog.

"Will somebody please tell that thing to SHUT THE FUCK UP!" Carlisle yelled.

Carlisle took three deep breaths. He had to get closer to see what he already knew was inside: the bloodied body of a young girl.

It did not take a police detective to know Kelly died long before the first ambulance arrived. The sheer amount of blood running through the crack between what remained of the passenger door and the rest of the car told Carlisle all he needed to know. The girl who could fend off monsters with her teeth met a monster she could not beat: her own mother.

Kelly was his to watch over, especially with Jimmy gone, and Carlisle failed. He would not sugarcoat that reality. He would do his best to keep it from eating him alive, but he would not edit this part out of his story. Ever.

The weight of the cell phone in his pocket and the call he knew only he could make drove him to the ground. His back slumped against the rear passenger tire. He closed his fists and silently screamed until his face ached. He dug his fingernails into the palms of his hands hard enough to draw blood. Carlisle cried until he dry-heaved, his body futilely trying to expel something that would always remain.

With her welfare benefits exhausted, Diane had become a full-time prostitute. Any money she earned came from selling her body. Carlisle was sure later they would find her in a trailer with Dakota Brady and a few of Roger Crowder's old crew, who would, undoubtedly, give Diane a place to lie down and a little crystal in exchange for a few minutes of her time.

That is exactly what happened.

The young officer who approached Carlisle at the scene and two other policemen found Diane with Brady. She was high, though her consumption of crystal meth in Brady's trailer presented a problem: No one could definitively prove if she was high when she was driving, or if she started using after she fled the scene of her daughter's death.

The timing of Diane's meth consumption was one mystery.

The other mystery was what Kelly was doing in a car headed toward Dakota Brady's trailer on a school night, after eleven PM. Carlisle had a theory, though he would keep it to himself. He wouldn't even tell Claudia.

Carlisle believed Diane asked Kelly to run an errand with her. Perhaps Diane promised Kelly a Slurpee and some Twizzlers if she went with her to get a fresh sixer of Milwaukee's Best. Carlisle knew Kelly was lonely, and maybe—against her better judgment—she decided to go with her mother to the store. Carlisle believed shortly after leaving their home, Diane told Kelly they were going to Dakota Brady's house instead.

Though Diane might not have said it in so many words, Kelly would have understood: her own mother intended to trade time with the unravaged body of her sixteen-year-old daughter in exchange for more and better meth, and a little money to help her make it through the next couple of weeks. Kelly might have also understood that Brady, with the consent of her mother, would love to put a little meth in her lungs to help ease her mind.

If Kelly realized this, she would have fought. The little girl who once bit her father's neck wasn't going down the same road her mother traveled without a fight. Kelly would have kicked at her mother, screamed at her, told her she wished she was dead before opening the passenger door to jump out. When Kelly went for the door handle Diane pressed down hard on the gas pedal, and almost immediately lost control of the vehicle.

Carlisle's theory was correct, but as the Department's lead detective, he officially concluded it was a tragic accident. A mistake. His decision no doubt influenced the judge's decision to accept Diane's Alford plea, which resulted in five years of probation and no prison time.

He did not want Jimmy to know his sister's last few moments were spent fighting their mother to keep her from doing to Kelly what she did to herself. The only thing left to give Jimmy that would last were memories unmarred by visions of a panicked, terrified Kelly.

Once word got back to the crash site that Diane had been taken into custody, Carlisle drove his cruiser to a spot overlooking the new and still unpopulated development where Jimmy taught Kelly to drive. Carlisle got out and leaned against the driver-side door. The air was even cooler, the night still clear. He dialed Jimmy's cell phone, which was a luxury he purchased so Kelly could call him any time. It took Carlisle three times to dial Jimmy's number without collapsing in dry heaves.

Almost a thousand miles away, in a dorm room in Tempe, Arizona, Jimmy saw Carlisle's number. It was late by then, past midnight even with the difference in time zones. Jimmy opened his phone on the first ring.

"Jimmy," Carlisle said.

When Carlisle dialed his friend after eleven o'clock and didn't begin the call with "my man," Jimmy's world collapsed. Carlisle said more words and no words and all those words were one word SORRYSORRYSORRYSORRYSORRYSORRY and Jimmy felt everything beneath his skin collapse, and collapse, and collapse, and collapse, and collapse and collapse and collapse and collapse and collapse oh my godOHMYGODOHMYGODOHMYGOD KELLYKELLYKELLYKELLYKELLYKELLYKELLYKELLYKELLYKELLY and collapse and collapse and collapse and collapse KELLYKELLYKELLYKELLYKELLYKELLYKELLY and inside his dorm room a black hole burst that swallowed all light and everything went dark and no lights all the bulbs popped and his lamp winked out and he never saw because it was already so dark especially inside and especially in his heart and KELLYKELLYKELLYKELLYKELLYKELLYKELLY FUCKINGDIANEFUCKINGDIANEFUCKINGDIANEFUCKINGDIANEFU CKINGDIANE—Jimmy lifted his neck and rammed his forehead against the linoleum as hard as he could, the sound like throwing a package of hamburger at a wall. Blood ran through cracks in the linoleum and sprayed—actually sprayed—the second time his forehead hit the floor.

He needed and wanted to bleed, just like Kelly had.

That's how his roommate found him, crying, bloody, and screaming into the floor. He was taken to the medical facilities on campus, where the nurse stitched up his forehead and diagnosed him with shock. The diagnosis was based on the look in Jimmy's eyes, and it was accurate. Fearing his self-harm would worsen, Jimmy was kept at the medical facility and released the next day when a police officer from Oklahoma called to see if someone on campus would drive Jimmy to the airport.

Jimmy's roommate packed a bag and drove him to Sky Harbor. Two hours later he landed in Oklahoma. Carlisle greeted him just past the new TSA security checkpoint, Jimmy still obviously in shock. He spent the next five days zombie-walking around Carlisle's house. Claudia tried to feed Jimmy as much as possible, even though he usually ended up vomiting a short while later.

Carlisle handled Kelly's cremation, including the payment. There was a memorial assembly at her high school. The band kids gathered in the multi-purpose room and played Kelly's favorite song, "Time after Time." They were unsure child musicians crying their way through something they couldn't really understand, and most couldn't make it through the whole song.

Jimmy sat through the memorial assembly and the small service held in Carlisle's backyard without saying a word. When he left for Arizona, the only tether connecting him to the rest of the world stretched as far as it could go. Now, with his sister nothing but dust, that tether snapped.

Those five days at Carlisle's house were Jimmy's last five days in Oklahoma.

He would never return.

His mother was tried for vehicular manslaughter, though the trial concluded when the judge accepted the Alford plea, which kept Diane from ever seeing the inside of a jail cell. The judge, in the sort of misplaced sympathy for terrible parents Carlisle hated, believed Diane Lansford had suffered enough. The judge's logic held that after the strange suicide of her beloved husband, it was no wonder she descended further into madness and addiction.

One of the conditions of her probation mandated rehab to treat her drug use. Diane moved from the home she shared with Jimmy and Kelly to a trailer outside of town, not far from where her husband committed suicide. The threat of jail did what being a mother could not: kept her off crystal, though she replaced the drug with even greater amounts of Milwaukee's Best.

A few years later, her probation officer found her in her trailer, dead from liver failure. She hadn't spoken to Jimmy since the day he left Oklahoma to return to ASU for his sophomore year. He didn't attend her trial and didn't care one way or another what became of his mother.

For the third time in less than a decade, Mike Carlisle responded to a scene with a dead Lansford. When he did, he picked up his cell phone and made a call.

"My man," he said.

When Carlisle informed him of Diane's death, Jimmy did not ram his head into the floor until he bled. He stood in his living room as Jill wrapped her arms around his shoulders, her pregnant belly against his back, his young son playing with small toy cars near his feet. Carlisle offered to handle the payment and logistics of the cremation, and though Jimmy accepted the help with logistics, this time he would not take Carlisle's money.

When his mother died, Jimmy was still in his mid-twenties. He was proud of many things: his education, his wife, his son, the baby girl on the way, how people didn't know where and who he came from. And when Carlisle offered to pay for Diane Lansford's cremation, Jimmy was proud he had enough money to personally send his mother into a scorching fire.

Part of him wanted to pay someone back in Oklahoma to dig up his father's body and burn it, too.

The day his mother's remains arrived, he took them straight to the storage unit in North Phoenix where he stored his other horrors, including his father's suicide note and Kelly's ashes.

A day after Kelly's funeral, Carlisle drove Jimmy back to the airport. He knew Jimmy didn't have any close friends in Arizona. The young man, for all intents and purposes, now lacked any family at all. The Lansfords who attended Kelly's service were distant cousins who came because they thought there might be free liquor—at a sixteen-year-old girl's funeral, hosted at the home of a police officer. Though it saddened Carlisle, if the choice was between relatives who came to funerals looking to scam free booze and no family at all, Jimmy was better off without anyone.

Mike Carlisle and Jimmy Lansford said their goodbyes near the new TSA security checkpoint at the Will Rogers Airport in Oklahoma City. This was as far as Carlisle could take Jimmy. He would go the rest of the way on his own. They stood side by side, looking through the security checkpoint and down toward the terminal. Carlisle could smell Cinnabon everywhere.

When Carlisle was a child, Will Rogers Airport was glamorous, a place symbolizing escape and adventure for a poor kid like him. Now it was just a place where you rewarded yourself for getting felt up by a TSA agent with a two-thousand-calorie cinnamon roll.

Things change, and not always for the better. It made Carlisle want to cry.

"Jimmy—"

Jimmy pulled Carlisle hard into his body, their cheeks banging together like a pair of mismatched black and white cymbals.

"Thank you," Jimmy said.

"Wh—Jimmy, I wish—"

"I know. I know what she meant to you. I know what we meant to you."

"Don't say 'meant,' Jimmy. This doesn't change anything. You hear me?" Carlisle grabbed the back of Jimmy's neck with his hand. "This doesn't change anything. You two still mean the world to me. I should have been a bigger part of her life, like I was with you."

Jimmy opened his eyes as wide as they would go, trying to dry them with stale airport air.

Deep down, no matter what they said to each other in the ticketing area of Will Rogers Airport, Jimmy knew he and Mike Carlisle were saying goodbye.

"You never had to do any of this," Jimmy said, his voice breaking. "Do you know what our lives would be like without you? I just wish...I wish—"

Carlisle knew what his friend was trying to say. Jimmy wished there was some way to pay Carlisle back. The two men stood, cheek to cheek, Carlisle's goatee prickly against Jimmy's skin. Carlisle kissed his friend, his lips lingering softly on Jimmy's stubble. Carlisle knew if he didn't use everything he had, including his touch, Jimmy could just float away, a balloon floating high and cold and alone, a balloon wishing for the moment it popped. They stood in that embrace, not caring who saw. Carlisle learned to do that from Jimmy and Kelly.

Carlisle whispered in his ear, "Turn around, go through that security gate, and never look back. Ever. Leave this place. If you need me, you have my number. But Jimmy, there's nothing here for you. Go build your life. Make your own family. Live a long life. I'm tired of you Lansfords dying."

As Carlisle spoke into his ear, Jimmy felt the detective's tears begin to pool in the space where their cheeks touched.

They stepped away from each other, and Carlisle placed his hands on Jimmy's shoulders.

"My man," he said. "Go."

Jimmy turned and went, first through the security checkpoint where he took off his shoes and walked through a metal detector. Jimmy picked up his bag after it passed inspection. Inside was a suit and a nice pair of shoes, packed by Claudia with Carlisle's permission. The clothes were men's clothes, but not because she bought them first for Carlisle in the men's section of a Dillard's in Oklahoma City. They were men's clothes because they first belonged to a man who looked for the best in people and took chances on them when he saw it, a man who made only promises he knew he could keep, a man who tried to choose right and owned the moments when he chose wrong, a man who never rewrote the ending to fit the choices he made in the middle.

Though it didn't fit right away, Jimmy grew into Carlisle's suit faster than he expected.

When he and Jill were just starting out, Jimmy wore that suit to every job interview he was invited to. He wore it the first time he ever made money trading a milk future, which was also the thousandth and best time he telepathically told the old owners of a long-abandoned Oklahoma dairy to fuck off. Two children, one wife, and two presidents later, the suit still hung in his closet. It was one of the few exceptions to Jimmy's rule and had never been banished to the storage unit. It was still, and always would be, a good fit.

Though the suit was old, it was well cared for, and such a part of Jimmy's wardrobe that it became part of him. He usually forgot where he got it—which, had he known, is exactly what Carlisle would have wanted.

After he picked up his bag, Jimmy turned and headed down the terminal. He did as Carlisle asked and didn't look back. Not even once.

It would be almost twenty years before the two men saw each other again.

CHAPTER SEVENTEEN

2019

Jill watched her husband from the doorway, his head bent over the bathroom sink. A few minutes earlier he walked upstairs, telling his family goodnight. Though he hadn't injured his legs during his afternoon run to Walmart, Jimmy limped ever since he returned home from the hospital three days ago. Jill couldn't say why, but she was pretty sure his limp would remain.

She knew what running meant to him but thought change would be a good thing. The kids were getting bigger. She would start her job as a CFO in a week. Jimmy, never one for change, could take baby steps. Instead of running, maybe he could take up weightlifting. Or CrossFit. Change didn't have to a be a disaster, especially if the alternative was running until you dropped dead.

"Hey babe," Jill said, embracing Jimmy from behind as he wiped the remaining toothpaste from his chin.

He put his arms over hers, keeping her just where she was for a few moments. She pressed her cheek into his back, then broke their embrace. Jimmy had been married a long time and knew being called "babe" was often the beginning of a long and important conversation.

Jimmy moved toward the toilet, setting the lid down and taking a seat. Jill turned around, her back to the mirror, and lifted herself onto the sink, where she faced Jimmy. They looked at each for a while, two people who knew each other far better than they knew themselves.

"So, are we going to talk about it?" Jill asked.

"Talk about what?"

"Jimmy. Are you serious?"

He took a breath and slowly exhaled. He knew this conversation was coming as soon as Jill felt he was healthy enough to have it.

"What do you want to know?"

"About what happened."

"You won't believe me."

"What? Why would I not believe you?"

Because you are a sensible person, Jimmy wanted to say. You have a degree in accounting and are going to be a CFO and good CFOs don't believe in ghosts or demons.

"Jimmy, I mean tell me about when you were a kid. I want to know more. About you. About my husband. I will believe you. Whatever you tell me. Plus, we're mortgage-official, so I legally have to believe you."

He looked up at her, confused.

"Mortgage official?" he asked.

"Yeah, it's like Facebook-official, but if you leave me I can take half your crap, Mr. Hotshot-Trader Man."

He laughed, and she winked, and he knew he would tell her what she deserved to hear.

"My childhood is just sad. Really sad."

"Then let me share it with you. Don't carry it alone."

For the next hour Jimmy gave her the details she always lacked. How his parents went from cocaine in the '80s to meth in the '90s. How he and Kelly never lived at the same address for more than a year until his father died. How he never, ever had a single friend over for a sleepover. How their kitchen counter was a kaleidoscope of cigarette burns, and so on some days were his forearms.

The burns were a secret he kept even from Carlisle, knowing it could set in motion a series of events that would place him and Kelly in separate homes.

A thousand maybes and a thousand more maybes branching off each of those, and in half of them Kelly might still be alive.

Though it pained him to see the expression on his wife's face as she heard what her husband and his little sister lived through, he knew this was the easy part of this conversation. After he told her all he could think to tell, he waited for the follow-up question.

"And what about now?" she asked, tossing a wet Kleenex toward the wastebasket.

It was a difficult shot from her angle, and when she banked it off the wall and into the wastebasket, Jimmy said, "So that's where he gets it from."

"Where who gets what from?"

"Jonathan. He must get his basketball skills from you."

"Not everything is passed from parent to child, Jimmy. Don't avoid my question, either. What's happening now, in our house?"

"Now?"

"Jimmy, you almost died."

Jimmy stared down at his bare feet, stalling for time, but he knew Jill would sit on the sink all night if she needed to. There was no other way out. He had to say it.

"I thought I was possessed by a demon."

Jill didn't laugh, didn't snicker, didn't tell her husband he was crazy. She just extended her right leg until her foot touched Jimmy's knee.

"When did you start to think this?" she asked.

"Well, when I was younger...when I was younger I started to think ...I thought for a while our parents were possessed by demons. Or something. Jill, I know—I know how this sounds."

"I don't think you're crazy, Jimmy." She pushed her foot harder against his knee. "Why did you stop thinking that? Was it what Kelly said about your parents being too big of losers for the devil to want them?"

"I grew up. I took Psych 101 and Abnormal Psychology as electives my junior year. I realized I was trying to rationalize the fact that my parents were terrible at being parents. I was okay with that explanation for years. And then it started."

"What started?"

Jimmy sighed.

"Remember my trip to Cedar Rapids?"

"Yeah. You texted me 'I'm safe.' It was weird. I just thought you were tired."

"That night I thought I saw someone in my room. There was a window that looked out on the hot tub. I thought I saw someone looking down on me. From the window. Well, security checked and there was no one. But there was a handprint on the window inside the room."

The hair on Jill's forearms prickled up.

"A handprint? Are you sure it wasn't there before?"

"I—" The thought never occurred to Jimmy. Was the handprint there before? Doesn't the cleaning crew wipe down the windows? He didn't know.

"What else?"

"I thought I felt something in the bathroom during Jessica's party. Pushing against me."

"What else?"

"In the storage unit I felt...I felt like I floated away. Far away."

Jill looked her husband in the eye, holding his gaze as she used a small rubber band to pull her hair into a nighttime ponytail. Jill was, in every way, the opposite of his mother. Educated and intelligent, her beauty came without sharp edges. More than anything, though, to Jimmy she embodied the most underrated sexy quality a human can possess: reliability.

"I don't know what to say, Jimmy. I mean—if anything in our lives is haunted, it might be the box in that storage unit. You should bring Kelly home, and get rid of the rest."

Jimmy said he would like that, though he would bring his old white Nikes home, too. He told her about the morning of the footprints and about being scared of getting taken back to Oklahoma, and how he couldn't bear the thought of returning to that place, even if it was just in his mind.

"But tell me, why did you jump out the window? Why did you run to Walmart?" Jill asked.

"Um—you're going to laugh."

"Laugh? None of this is funny, Jimmy."

"I ran to get a Ouija board. They only had one, and this cashier did a price check in front of the whole store."

The sound of Jill's laugh relaxed Jimmy.

Jimmy confessed everything except the dry run with the screwdriver. In a marriage, honesty is almost always the best policy. Jimmy knew that. But there had to be exceptions, he thought, and one of those exceptions was sharing too many details about the sharp end of a screwdriver in a family with a history of suicide.

"Do you still think there's something here?" Jill asked.

Jimmy looked around the room, glancing at the mirror.

"No," he said.

"Why not?"

"Because after that day, I haven't felt it. It's gone." He looked back at the mirror before locking eyes with Jill. "Or I imagined it. I was having a breakdown. I think I knew, in the back of my mind, that Jessica turning twelve would be hard. It was bad before Ronnie died. But it was worse after that. Diane, our mother, I mean, she turned the hate in both of our parents' hearts on us. And then..."

And then she killed Kelly, he wanted to say. After I left her behind.

The simple math of that—Jimmy left, and Kelly died, and she wouldn't have been in the car if he stayed in Oklahoma—was unavoidable and irrefutable. Jimmy would not let anyone tell him otherwise, believing if the truth can eat you alive, you deserve to get eaten. It was a far more brutal version of Carlisle's approach to Kelly's death.

Jill stood from the sink and said, "Wait here just a minute. I have something I want to show you." She left the bathroom, leaving Jimmy alone. He thought about standing up to see if there were any smudges in the mirror, but decided he was better off where he sat.

Jill re-entered the bathroom, holding a plastic grocery bag.

"Open it," she said, placing the bag and its contents at Jimmy's feet. Inside were a pair of filthy Kyrie Irving shoes caked in dry mud.

"What?" He asked, lifting one shoe out and inspecting it. One of the remaining pieces of dirt fell to the bathroom floor.

"It was Jonathan. He told me while you were in the hospital. The footprints were his fault. He was trying to clean up his mess when you got back."

"Why would he—"

"Lie to you, Jimmy? He wasn't lying. He just didn't want to let you down. No one wants to let you down."

"Is he afraid of me?"

Jill looked at him with the same stern look she used on their children.

"Jimmy, you are not your father. Or your mother. Do you hear me? No one is afraid of you. He just didn't want to disappoint you."

Jimmy looked at the filthy pair of one-hundred-dollar shoes sitting on his clean bathroom floor.

Jill kneeled down, her eyes locked on his.

"I want to say something, and you need to hear me."

"I—"

"Stop. Just listen," she said, waving a hand with a ring finger that sparkled with the world's least pawnable piece of jewelry.

"Okay."

"Jimmy, you are not possessed. It wasn't the devil. Or a ghost. The first twenty years of your life were awful because you and Kelly had awful parents. I don't—awful isn't even the right word. Listen to me: You didn't deserve what happened to you. Either of you."

"I know."

"No, you don't know. If you knew I wouldn't be learning brand new information after being married to you for this long. If you knew, you wouldn't have almost died."

She moved her hands to his cheeks, her wedding ring making a slight scratching sound as it brushed his stubble.

"You are not possessed. You are not a haunted man. You are not bad. You didn't deserve this. Neither did she. And Jimmy?"

"Yeah?"

"Look at your life," Jill said, motioning at the bathroom walls with her hands. "People are jealous of what you—of what we have. Have you ever been anything but successful in your career?"

"Jill—"

"Answer my question."

"No. I mean, yes. I've always been successful."

"And you have a beautiful family and a beautiful home with a wife and children who adore you. You spend so much time avoiding your past you sometimes forget to see what's in front of you."

"I'll be better."

Jill sighed. She didn't want Jimmy to promise to do better, like he wasn't keeping up on his portion of the housework.

"This isn't dirty dishes left in the sink. I'm not asking you to fix something for me. I'm telling you the universe or God or whatever is usually fair. Maybe, as awful as it was, that house and those burns were the price you paid for the life you live now."

Though Jill was trying to comfort him, her observation on the universe's inherent fairness broke Jimmy. When the tears came, they came with gasps and choking sounds and what Jessica would call a good hard ugly cry.

Through the tears Jimmy managed to ask Jill a question.

"What about Kelly? What does she get for the price she paid?"

It was a question deserving an answer, though it wasn't an answer Jill could give. She could tell him our reward for suffering so much might come in the next life, but she knew saying something like that wouldn't do any good. The next life is a long way away when you have to spend so many years in this life apart from someone you love.

Jill sensed a presence in the doorway.

Jonathan and Jessica were standing there, their images reflected in the bathroom mirror. She turned and waved her children in.

An observer who witnessed this scene might describe it as a moment of tremendous sorrow, a man weeping for his long-dead sister after having almost killed himself, surrounded by people gravely concerned about his well-being.

But family?

Anyone who belonged to a family like the one gathered around Jimmy Lansford would know differently. Family would know how important this hug was, that being touched in times of heartbreak was often what keeps a person from just floating away, from becoming a black balloon waiting for the day it can pop.

Jimmy constructed his entire life so he would never feel lost, never float away, never make his children feel as though they were being raised by an unstable parent. Their dad crying, giving in to the strength of his wife, was a new sight for Jonathan and Jessica.

It was so new and unexpected they all missed the way the digital clock on the bathroom kept glowing brighter and brighter as the Lansford family sequel squeezed each other tighter and tighter.

CHAPTER EIGHTEEN

August 2001

The backseat of the Camry was piled high with garbage bags full of clothes and a white pair of Nikes Jimmy had long since outgrown. If he left Garrity by noon, and drove all night, he would be back in Arizona by early the next afternoon.

First though, he had to fulfill two promises, both food-related. The first was his promise to have pancakes with Carlisle and his fiancée at their home. There was no limit to the number of pancakes Claudia could make, which was good, because there was no limit to the number of pancakes Jimmy could eat. After two hours of breakfast and talking about Jimmy's upcoming cross-country season, Carlisle gave Jimmy a hard handshake and said, "My man. You coming back for Thanksgiving?"

"You know I don't—"

Carlisle waved his hand, dismissing Jimmy's objection. In a month or two he would call Jimmy and tell him some old teammate worked at an airline, and he had called in a favor to get Jimmy on a flight to Oklahoma City. Jimmy shook Carlisle's hand, and then got back in the car, needing to get to his next and most important goodbye before he left town.

Jimmy waved goodbye to Claudia and Carlisle and headed for Derry's.

Kelly was waiting for him at one of the tables out front. She wore one of Jimmy's old cross-country shirts from high school, her hair in a ponytail. He parked in a space near her table and got out of the Camry. It was still early— not even noon—and the line to the Derry's window was short. Jimmy ordered two vanilla cones and brought them back, sitting next to Kelly on the same side of the bench. Across the street stood a liquor store, a convenience store, another liquor store, and three payday lenders. Every summer that was Jimmy's view as he worked and saved nearly every penny he earned.

The two sat in silence for a while, eating ice cream. Kelly placed her head on Jimmy's shoulder. Across the street a couple exited one of the payday lenders and entered a liquor store. Jimmy and Kelly did not judge. In the class structure of their neighborhood, these folks existed at least a few rungs higher than Diane. At least they had a steady paycheck they could use to repay the lender.

Kelly looked up at her brother, and said, "Motherfucker don't want none of this."

This time though, the motherfucker was Jimmy, and he knew it. He laughed, though he was scared Kelly would think she was part of what he wanted none of.

"Kelly, you know—"

She turned to face her brother.

"I know. Jimmy, I know."

"Next year, right? You'll be seventeen. Mom won't fight it."

"An apartment. An apartment with a pool," she said.

Jimmy laughed. He was old enough to drive a thousand miles by himself, but still young enough to believe a thousand-mile ribbon of blacktop was all it took to heal an ugly scar.

"It will get better, Kelly. A school year goes by fast. Before you know it, you'll live with me."

Kelly closed her eyes and thought of living with her brother in an actual, real city. With mountains. No more flat, dusty Oklahoma. Just mountains and swimming pools and anonymity. She could just be Kelly, the new girl at school who lives with her brother. Or she could be no one, just another person in a city full of people who came from somewhere else.

Either way, life after Diane sounded like heaven.

"Oh, hey!" Jimmy said. "I forgot. I have something for you."

"Yeah?"

"Yeah. Hang on."

Jimmy stood and walked to the Camry, where he reached through the rear window and pulled out a plastic grocery bag. He carried the bag back and sat next to Kelly, pulling out a used Polaroid camera. He'd seen it in the window of a pawn shop on his way home from a shift at Derry's a week ago.

"Take pictures and send them to me."

"What pictures should I take? The view around here," she said, gesturing to the businesses across the street, "pretty much sucks."

"I don't care what it is. Make some cookies and watch *Friends* and send pictures to me."

"Jimmy, I—this is cool. Thank you so much."

Kelly felt the weight of her camera in her hands. It was substantial, real, and would never end up back at a pawn shop.

She knew she had to hide it from their mother.

Jimmy took the camera from her hands and said, "Sit still." He stood from their bench, turning around to point the camera at Kelly. He looked at his sister through the viewer but didn't take the photo. He moved the camera away from his face and set it back down on the bench. He grabbed what remained of his ice cream cone, and before she could stop him, wiped a bit of vanilla on the tip of her chin.

"Hey!" Kelly said, but she laughed as she said it. She was smiling, ice cream on the end of her chin, looking like she was going to stand up and punch Jimmy when he took the picture. The insides of the camera whirred and produced a photo that Jimmy would one day frame and place on an expensive countertop in Phoenix.

"I'm going to keep this one," he said.

"You better not show anyone that."

"I won't," he said, though he knew it was going on the mini fridge in his dorm room, where some boy would inevitably ask about the girl in the picture.

"I love you so much," Kelly said.

"I love you too," Jimmy said.

"Love you, Ross," she said, kicking his foot.

"Love you too, Monica," he said, kicking back.

This second time Jimmy left Oklahoma without his sister wouldn't be any easier than the first. He was happy about that. If it got easier to leave her even once, it just might get easier to leave her altogether—to put her in a box of crap labeled "Oklahoma" and just get on with his life.

They stood together, knowing it was time to say goodbye. They hugged each other tight. Growing up, Ronnie and Diane only touched their children in anger. Hugs and heads on the shoulder were all the physical affection Jimmy and Kelly got, and they had to get it from each other. That, and a backslap and half-hug from Carlisle—which was good too.

"I love you, Kelly."

"I love you too, Jimmy. I'll miss you."

"I'll miss you, too."

Jimmy looked out over the top of his sister's head at the neighborhood she was still forced to call home. Anyone who never lived in a place like this viewed the families who go in and out of payday lenders as victims or users. Jimmy knew it wasn't so simple. The two people responsible for his and Kelly's existence were both.

"Hey! I forgot to tell you. I'm coming back for Thanksgiving!"

"Really? How?"

"Carlisle will help."

"Why don't you call him Mike?"

Jimmy thought about it.

"I don't know. I don't like calling mom and dad...mom and dad. You know? At school when I—if I talk about them, they're Ronnie and Diane. Carlisle—I like calling him by something more than just Mike. I tried Detective Carlisle once, but he hated that. So, it's just Carlisle."

Kelly punched her brother in the shoulder and leaned in for another hug.

"You think too much," she said.

Jimmy kissed his sister once on the top of the head, then walked toward the Camry.

"Bye, Jimmy."

"Bye, Kelly."

"See you for Thanksgiving!" Kelly yelled, waving one hand. Her Polaroid sat on the bench. Jimmy looked at her and wrinkled his nose. Hide that, his nose said, or mom will pawn it. It didn't need to be shouted across the parking lot.

Their signal was good enough.

Jimmy got in the Camry and backed out of his parking spot, waving once more as he turned onto the street. Outside his window, he passed places the motherfucker wanted none of: smoke shops, pawn shops, a strip club, vacant buildings with plywood windows. He looked in his rearview mirror once. Kelly took photos of the Camry as it drove away. Seeing his sister fade from view, Jimmy Lansford tried not to cry.

Jimmy Lansford did not succeed.

CHAPTER NINETEEN

2019

On the living room floor of an expensive home on the edge of Phoenix, illuminated by the softly pulsing light of a large television, sleeps a family of four. The parents lie next to one another. The dad's head rests on the mom's shoulder as the two hold each other tight.

It is the same way they held each other the first time they spent the night together.

Next to them lie their son and daughter, fifteen and twelve years old. Though the two siblings love each other, they do not have the intense bond the father once had with his sister.

They don't need to.

A real, complete family lives in this home, and the love needs to be spread around. No one has ever had to defend one family member from another. The only time anyone has hid anywhere to avoid being found by a parent was during a game of hide-and-seek, and even then, Jimmy, Jonathan, and Jessica stopped playing long enough to help Jill get out from under the kitchen sink.

After Jimmy stopped crying in the bathroom, Jill made them a family floor bed—something they hadn't done since Jonathan and Jessica were much younger. They turned on their favorite show, and Jessica fell asleep with her head next to her brother's shoulder, a Twizzler straw standing in an inch of warm Mountain Dew next to her.

Observing her family, her presence visible by the varying brightness of the television and a reflected smudge on the sliding glass door, Kelly

Lansford saw the resemblance—a resemblance that would still exist if Diane hadn't smashed the Firebird into a tree in a front yard in Oklahoma. Here, in Phoenix, there were no front yards. Just rock and cactus.

Kelly liked that.

But the connection between Kelly and Jessica was about more than just hair color and a nose that could wrinkle. Kelly knew she was part of Jessica, and Jessica a part of her, woven together by something older and more lovely than just a double-helix.

She didn't understand how she got here, but when she heard her brother cry she came running—just like he always had. She first found Jimmy in a room in the nicest hotel she had ever been in. She just wanted her big brother to know someone was keeping watch, even when he was so far from his family. Later she saw Jimmy staring at his own eye at the birthday party, and had come again, trying to mimic the hugging-from-behind thing she saw her brother's wife do.

The storage unit was another matter altogether. Though she loved her brother, she was angry when she saw her ashes in the same box with their mother's remains and their father's suicide note. She understood better than most the body was just a vessel and dust was just dust, but she would not be just another one of Jimmy Lansford's Oklahoma nightmares.

Kelly's dust did not need to be on the mantle, but she deserved better than a dark and lonely storage unit.

While she had nothing to do with the footprints, she did try to take part of Jimmy back to Oklahoma, but not to see any home they ever lived in. She wanted to take the essential part of Jimmy Lansford—the same part of Kelly that still existed—to the living room of Mike Carlisle as he planned a Thanksgiving trip to Phoenix. Carlisle was excited to see the little brother he hadn't seen years, and she wanted to show Jimmy how much this man still loved him.

She wanted to show her brother that not everything and everyone from their childhood was worth forgetting.

In a couple of months, Carlisle would be at this house for Thanksgiving, and so would Kelly. This was her family. This would be her home now, too. She would take up residence in the attic, coming down to check on her people when they needed checking on.

What they never commented on, but all felt, was the way their hearts occasionally pulsed brighter, and not the red-fibered muscles in their rib cages responsible for pumping blood, but the unchartered part of the human mind that could—with the right jolt of electricity—expand and expand and expand until they all—especially Jimmy—understood real love could never end with an anguished scream in the front yard of an abandoned Oklahoma meth house. Real love never ends with anything—no matter how final the illusion of an ending may seem—because real love simply never ends. Ever.

While Kelly would learn to be less intrusive than she had been over the past few weeks, she could still be useful. In her brief time living in her new home, she had learned how to set off car alarms and hide screwdrivers. She didn't have eyes in the way one typically thinks of eyes, but Kelly saw the knife rack on the kitchen counter. Though she thought her brother would be okay, if Jimmy started pointing one at his eye, she would hide the knives.

Kelly Lansford was where she always wanted to be: in a big home, with a pool, in an actual city, living with her big brother and being part of a real family.

Her real family.

She would watch these children grow, and one day she, Jill, and Jimmy would watch those children's children grow.

Together.

As the air outside the home cooled down to what could decently be called a fall temperature, at least in Phoenix, her family slept on the floor. The TV was still on, glowing ever brighter. A character on the show looked at the camera and said, "My, how the turntables have turned"—and then the television winked out.

The least she could do was try and mitigate her impact on their electricity bill—though, if countertops were any indication, her brother could easily afford having Kelly around.

More than anything, Kelly was proud. It did not look like she hoped it would, but Jimmy had done it. He had figured a way out of the hole—even if he sometimes slipped, temporarily, back in.

In his sleep Jimmy Lansford smiled. He smiled because he always loved that line about turntables, and even in his sleep he understood the line was a lot more than just a joke.

But the way he wrinkled his nose when he smiled?

He wrinkled his nose because fifteen feet away, as the display on his stainless steel oven glowed a deep, warm blue, a photo of a young girl with ice cream on her chin slid across a kitchen counter until it was next to a photo of the four people lying on the floor, the frames close enough to touch.

~End~

ACKNOWLEDGEMENTS

I have to say thank you six times before the close of this book.

The first and biggest thank you goes to my wife, Megan. She served as a beta-reader and editor—even though this book borrows a significant portion of Ronnie Lansford's suicide from the tragic, unexplainable, and violent suicide of her own father. In the aftermath of her loss she has shown courage, resilience, and bravery that is often unfathomable. She's also the love of my life, and a constant inspiration.

The second thank you goes to my brothers, Cody and Levi. To this day, if you take on one of us, you take on all of us—so be warned that a Facebook fight with one McKissen is a Facebook fight with all McKissens. Reviewers take heed. You have been warned.

The third thank you goes to my children: Elizabeth, Dylanger, and Colette. Everything I do, I do to impress the three of you. Thank you for the inspiration and the motivation. I love the three of you more than you will ever know.

The fourth thank you goes to the editors of this novel: Susan Rooks, Laura Novak, and John Baltisberger. Each of you made this book stronger and better.

The fifth thank you goes to Reagan Rothe and Black Rose Writing. Not every publisher would take a chance on a horror novel written by a business journalist and consultant. Independent presses like Black Rose take chances on writers, not business models. Thank you for taking a chance on me.

Finally, thank you to anyone who has ever read my writing, regardless the format or platform. All those likes and shares of my business blogs gave me the courage to pursue a dream I thought had died a long time ago. I hope to earn your continued support, and hopefully a royalty check here and there. It isn't much, but dinner for five at Applebee's doesn't pay for itself.

Dustin McKissen
May 7, 2019

NOTE FROM THE AUTHOR

Word-of-mouth is crucial for any author to succeed. If you enjoyed the book, please leave a review online—anywhere you are able. Even if it's just a sentence or two. It would make all the difference and would be very much appreciated.

Thanks!
Dustin

ABOUT THE AUTHOR

Dustin McKissen is an award-winning writer for a variety of publications. In addition to his non-fiction writing, Dustin is the author of the novel *The Civil War at Home* and the award-winning short stories *Wife Number Six* and *My Name is Theodore Robert Bundy, and I am a Nixon Man*. He lives in St. Charles, Missouri with his wife Megan and their three children. Dustin is a graduate of Prescott College and Northern Arizona University.

Facebook – https://www.facebook.com/DMcKissen/
Twitter – @DMcKissen
LinkedIn – https://www.linkedin.com/in/dustin-mckissen-53007056

Thank you so much for reading one of our **Horror** novels.

If you enjoyed our book, please check out our recommended title for your next great read!

Doll House by John Hunt

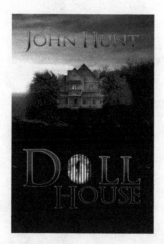

"Olivia. She's a brilliant character, broken, but trying to survive on her terms." -*Ginger Nuts of Horror*

"The female lead, Olivia, is a great character. She reminded me of Jamie Lee Curtis." -*Cedar Hollow Horror Reviews*

"It is certainly shocking and gruesome, but John Hunt manages it quite impressively." -*The Novel Pursuit*

View other Black Rose Writing titles at www.blackrosewriting.com/books and use promo code **PRINT** to receive a **20% discount** when purchasing.